UNTANGLE ME

TENTH ANNIVERSARY EDITION

www.chellebliss.com

CHELLE BLISS

USA TODAY BESTSELLING AUTHOR

www.chellebliss.com

CHELLE BLISS

USA TODAY BESTSELLING AUTHOR

Dear Fellow Bookworm,

Over ten years ago, I decided to put pen to paper and see what would happen. Never in my wildest dreams could I imagine that it would lead to a writing career with over sixty novels and thousands of new friends.

Even to this day, I'm still amazed when someone loves my words and the characters I've created. I write for the sheer joy of it, the creativity of dreaming up happy worlds filled with love and laughter.

Many of you have been with me on this whacky journey filled with so many ups and downs. You've been patient, supportive, and at times...the thing that keeps me tapping away on the keyboard even in my darkest moments.

I can't thank you enough for everything over the years. Over the next ten, twenty, or thirty years, I hope to create many more stories for you to devour.

This book was my start. It's not the prettiest, but we all start somewhere. From this story, the Men of Inked was born...

Much Love,

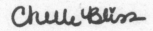

CHELLE BLISS

Dear Fellow Bookworm,

Over ten years ago I decided to put pen to paper and see what would happen. Never in my wildest dreams could I imagine that it would lead to a writing career with over sixty novels and thousands of new friends.

Even to this day, I'm still amazed when someone loves my words and the characters I've created. I write for the sheer joy of it—the creativity of dreaming up happy worlds filled with love and laughter.

Many of you have been with me on this wacky journey filled with so many ups and downs. You've been patient, supportive and at times, the thing that keeps me tapping away on the keyboard even in my darkest moments.

I can't thank you enough for everything over the years. Over the next ten...twenty, or thirty years, I hope to create many more stories for you to devour.

This book was my start. I'll spare the preface, but we all start somewhere. Read this story, the start of it all, where it all was born.

Much love,

Chelle Bliss

Originally Published © 1st October 2013
Fifth Edition Copyright © June 2017
Editing: Silently Correcting Your Grammar
Cover Design © Mooney Designs

www.chellebliss.com
CHELLE BLISS
USA TODAY BESTSELLING AUTHOR

To my parents... I'd be nothing without your love.

sophia

"HELLO..." he said. "Earth to Sophia."

I jumped as fingers snapped in my face. "Oh, sorry, Gary." I blinked a couple of times, trying to focus.

"Where did you go?"

"Nowhere, something just caught my eye on the other side of the restaurant." I'd always been a terrible liar, but thank God Gary was too self-absorbed to even care.

He asked me out six months ago after work. I figured, what the hell, why not? He was attractive, a couple years younger, had a stable job, and seemed reliable.

"As I was saying before you zoned out, this kid in my class today..."

I stared at him but couldn't comprehend a word he spoke. I didn't try to either. I wanted to leave work behind at the end of the day, but Gary couldn't talk about anything else.

We had a casual relationship, going out once a week for dinner and drinks. But lately, the evenings ended at his place and consisted of lackluster sex and mind-numbing conversation.

Gary was the type of man who "made love" in the only position he was comfortable...missionary. I moaned when it seemed right and faked my orgasms when I'd had enough.

Sex with Gary just didn't have that extra something that pulled me over the edge. But then again, I'd never found anyone who gave it to me that way.

"Can you believe he said that?" Gary laughed.

If people could be a color, Gary would be gray. He didn't have the edginess to be black or the sparkle of white. He was perfectly gray—dull, lifeless, and totally bland.

I laughed, shaking my head and playing along. "That's too funny." My insides were dying from boredom as I spun the pasta around my fork for a little excitement.

"Do you want to come over tonight?" He raised an eyebrow, and that was his way of asking if I felt like "making love."

Fuck, fuck, fuck.

Why can't he just say it? I wanted a man who would pull my hair, spank my ass, and make me come so hard I saw stars. Instead, I had gray Gary with his adequate-size cock and no clue how to use it.

"I'm kind of tired. Do you mind if I take a rain check?"

His toothy smile vanished. "Another night, then," he replied, glancing down at his pasta and stabbing at the noodles.

I tried to pay attention the rest of dinner, but I barely heard a word he said. I nodded when it was right, laughed when he did, and said a silent prayer when it was all over.

When he kissed me good-bye and closed my car door, I could tell he was upset, but I wasn't going to spend another night with gray Gary in missionary position with no satisfaction.

As I pulled into my driveway, I sighed at the thought of another Friday night alone in my pajamas. I wanted to crawl out of my skin, break the good-girl mold I'd allowed others to cage me in. I lived another life in my books, one filled with excitement and passion. My book boyfriends dominated me, fucking me so hard that the orgasms knocked me out just like the lucky bitches in the books.

A notification flashed across my phone screen just as I crawled into bed, curling up with my flavor of the week. Tonight, I'd have my hair pulled and ass smacked by an alpha male with a heart.

My eyebrows drew together, and I chewed on my lip as I stared at the name. Kayden Michaels wanted to be my friend on Facebook. His name didn't sound familiar, but I clicked on his profile anyway out of curiosity.

He grew up close to my hometown and we had a few mutual friends, but not even his face looked familiar. One thing I learned working in a school, never blindly hit accept unless I knew the person. Too many students, both current and former, were trying to find out about my life, and some things were meant to be kept private.

Me: Do I know you?

I studied his face again as I waited for his reply. He had warm green eyes, a shaved head, a sinful grin framed by a goatee, and dimples.

Fucking hell, he's got dimples.

His facial hair was a mix of brown and gold, but the rest of him was smooth and hairless, well, at least the parts I could see. He looked like the quintessential bad boy, a type I steered clear of my entire life but visited nightly in my fantasies.

I tapped my finger against my bottom lip, my finger hovering over the decline button before his message stopped me.

Kayden: Not yet.

I leaned back on my pillow, trying to figure out if he was an asshole or if the line was clever.

Kayden: I saw your post to Freddie, we went to school together.

Freddie was a lifelong family friend, my brother's

best friend throughout childhood. He went on vacations with us, attended holidays, and became a second brother to me.

Me: Freddie's a friend of my brother's.

Kayden: I don't remember you hanging out with us back in the day.

Butterflies filled my stomach as I thought about my brother's friends. I had a crush on most of them during my awkward teenage years, but they treated me like a pesky little sister. I wanted to tag along and be included in everything they did, but I usually ended up being discarded from their plans and left behind.

Me: I'm younger and didn't really hang out with them.

Kayden: Probably for the best...at least for you, but not for me.

I smiled at his small flirtation. My brother's friends had flirting down pat and had girls dropping their panties from just a smile.

Me: It was best for me at the time. Thanks for the request, maybe we'll talk again sometime.

Kayden: Hey, wait! Where ya going?

I chewed on my lip as I typed a response and then erased it. I didn't want to explain that all I wanted to do was get lost in a great book. Not to a hot guy who probably could put every single book boyfriend to shame.

Me: Well, I figured we were finished talking.

I winced as I read over my message. I couldn't

think of anything witty, and while he was being playful, I'd become gray Gary.

Kayden: I'm not. Are you wild like your brother?

That was laughable to anyone who truly knew me. My brother lived differently, never taking the easy road. He led a rebellious life filled with adventure and danger. I read books, attended college, and fucked only a handful of guys in my entire life. We were polar opposites.

Me: Although I love him, we're nothing alike. You?

The last thing I needed was to talk to someone from my brother's crazy world. I'd always steered clear of any type of trouble, and not even a pretty face would change that.

Kayden: Hell no! I wrestled with them but never hung out with them.

Me: Smart boy.

Kayden: Boy? It's been a long time since someone called me that, li'l girl.

I smirked at his reply because I'd always had a thing for that cute pet name.

Me: LOL. Tell me about Kayden "the man."

Kayden: I'll give you the short version of my life. I live in New Orleans, install cable, I'm thirty-six, work hard, play harder, and am blissfully single. You?

Me: I'm a school librarian, live in Florida, divorced. I'm thirty-two, and I'm navy blue verging on gray.

I chuckled, hitting the send button. My message

was cryptic, and I knew he wouldn't understand, but it was the truth.

Kayden: What the hell does that mean?

Soon, I'd be giving gray Gary a run for his money in the boring department if I didn't do something to change it.

Me: Nothing, just an inside joke. Hey, I'm tired. Maybe we can talk again soon.

Kayden: We will. I have to be up early for work anyway. Sweet dreams, beautiful.

My cheeks warmed with his words—beautiful. I'd been called beautiful before but usually not by a man I'd classify as out of my league. Oh, don't get me wrong. I knew I was cute, but in that bookish, nerdy girl way without the thigh highs and sexy kitten heels.

Me: Night.

What the fuck did I just do?

A sexy man was flirting with me, and I ran away like a scared schoolgirl. So lame. I sighed as I relaxed into my cushy headboard, opened my book and began reading, but I pictured Kayden and his sparkling green eyes looking into mine as I read every dirty word.

I hadn't been able to get Kayden off my mind. I'd wanted to message him since the moment I woke up, but I couldn't find the nerve.

I checked him out, making sure he wasn't a crazy

person. When I didn't find any red flags, I did the only thing I could to find out more about Kayden and hopefully get rid of the butterflies that filled my stomach every time I thought about him. I messaged Freddie.

Me: Hey, Freddie. Question for you—do you know Kayden Michaels?

Freddie: Yeah, we went to school together. Why?

I bit my nail, trying to think of how to answer this without it getting back to my brother. He'd throw a shit fit. I might be older and wiser—he'd debate that fact—but he still had the ability to send guys running for the hills for even looking in my direction.

Me: He sent me a friend request. I wanted to know if he was an asshole.

Freddie: Nah, kid. He's a good guy. Did you talk to him?

Me: Not really, just wanted to make sure it's okay to accept his friend request.

Freddie: Yeah, go for it. If he gives you any shit, you tell me and I'll handle it.

Me: Always, Freddie. Thanks!

Freddie had given him the stamp of approval. I just needed to get the courage to send him a message. I turned the phone over in my hand, pacing back and forth like I was been possessed.

Kayden: Morning, Sophia. Sleep well?

Oh. My. Fucking. God.

Did he know I was stalking him? Did Freddie say something to him?

Concentrate on breathing... *Inhale and exhale, slowly.*

Me: Hey, yeah... I slept well, and you?

I should just crawl into a hole or bang my head against the wall because I couldn't have sounded any more boring.

Kayden: Slept like a baby. What did you mean last night about being navy blue?

I twirled my hair around my finger and thought of a way to explain it without sounding like a deranged lunatic.

Me: Is navy blue an exciting color?

I rolled my eyes at my stupidity. *Shit.* I fidgeted, waiting for his response. I was a librarian and should have a way with words, but when it came to men, I lost all ability to speak and never sounded eloquent.

Kayden: Umm, not really.

Me: Well, it's the color of my life.

I glanced around my office, wondering if anyone could see me blush, but the library was empty and the kids hadn't started to pile in yet.

Kayden: Impossible.

Me: Entirely true.

Kayden: Come on! You're Mike's sister, and you're hot as hell. No way you're boring.

My belly flipped at "hot as hell." It made my skin prickly, but in a sexy, spine-tingling way.

Me: I'm nothing like my brother, Kayden. I learned what not to do by watching him.

Kayden—even his name wasn't bland.

Kayden: I never thought you were. You just share DNA. That doesn't make you navy blue. Tell me more about yourself. Are you seeing anyone?

How much should I tell him? I'd never meet him. I'd read the stories about women being abducted and never heard from again. I didn't know the man behind the message. Freddie knew him in school, but so many things changed as we get older. He could be a total creeper with a side of serial killer, and no one would be the wiser.

Me: I'm seeing someone casually. He's a nice guy.

Kayden: That's the kiss of death.

Me: What is?

Kayden: Being a nice guy. It's code for he sucks.

I snickered at the spot-on interpretation of Gary. It's exactly what I meant without coming right out and saying it.

Me: He doesn't suck. It's not easy to find someone to fit my perfect mold.

Kayden: I thought I found "the one" twice in my life. I've abandoned trying and stopped dating altogether.

Why were all the hot guys unavailable? It left single ladies like me to drown in a sea of gray and turning to our fictional men for companionship.

Me: I can't give up, not yet at least.

Kayden: Why did you end up divorced? If I can ask. I don't want to offend you.

Leaning back in my chair, I tapped my foot against

the carpet and thought about how I'd explain every-thing that happened—or didn't happened, I should say.

Me: So many things went wrong. I met him right after high school, and we married years later. The relationship lacked in so many ways, but I ignored them, waiting for things to change.

A lump formed in my throat thinking about my past failure. I thought I'd be with him forever and that we'd have a family and grow old together. I couldn't have been more wrong, but it was me who asked for the divorce. I couldn't accept the mundane existence that was my marriage.

Kayden: Lacked how?

I sipped on my coffee, waiting for his reply and thought back on how unhappy I was back then. One day it was like a lightbulb switched on, and I realized I couldn't take another day just existing together. I wanted the love I read about. I wanted the romance. I wanted a partner and not a friend.

Me: I felt more like a roommate and his housekeeper. Totally passionless. There was no romance. We talked about having kids, but it would've been a miracle.

Kayden: Was he gay?

I spat out my coffee, drenching my desk as I read his message. The thought had crossed my mind a time or two, especially since he was never particularly interested in sex.

Me: No. We weren't right for each other, and I had to walk away.

Kayden: All that long brown hair, big beautiful brown eyes, and with that smokin' hot body. How can a man not want to fuck you?

I blinked more than once, rereading his message. He'd said I was beautiful again.

Kayden: A relationship is nothing without passion. You made the right choice. It's not always easy, but it's best to keep your sanity.

I didn't want the conversation to be about me anymore. I wasn't looking for compliments and didn't need to open old wounds that had already healed. I wanted to know about him, about Kayden, and what made him tick.

Me: You've given up on dating entirely?

Kayden: Yes, strictly physical relationships now.

I'd be lying if I didn't admit that his statement disappointed me for some odd reason. It's not like I was going to run out and throw myself in his arms, but it would've been nice to know it was a possibility.

Me: So...you have sex with strangers? Are you that guy —the type who sleeps with a girl, never to be heard from again?

What other type could he be? Really, I'm not different. I don't sleep with men I don't know, but I've slept with Gary, and I wouldn't call him my boyfriend by any stretch of the word.

Kayden: Fuck no, not anymore at least. I'm upfront with each of them.

Each of them? Did that mean he's sleeping with more than one?

Me: Them?

Kayden: I'm not banging my way through the female population of New Orleans, but I turn to a couple girls I know in my times of need.

A porno clip played in my mind, and he was the star with his rockin' body and hard cock, doing what he just claimed he didn't. I fanned myself, heat crawling up my neck because the thought of him fucking anyone turned me on.

Kayden: I'm not a dick about it.

I blinked, being pulled out of my sex haze and realizing I needed to get a goddamn grip. I've been basically celibate for so long that a man I'd typically run in the opposite direction from now turns me on.

Me: You sound kind of like a caveman to me.

Kayden: I don't take what's not freely offered. They know I'll never be their boyfriend. They take it for what it is, a night of pleasure...mind-numbing pleasure. The type that makes your toes curl, takes your breath away, and leaves you wanting more.

Every part of my body ignited. I'd never had that...ever.

I wanted it more than anything in the world. The bland vanilla sex in my real life lacked the passion and want of the carnal pleasure I had with my book boyfriends.

Me: OMG. You're a manwhore.

Kayden: Ouch, Sophia. That's a bit harsh, isn't it?

Me: I thought it was more funny than harsh. I meant it in the nicest way.

I didn't blame Kayden.

I'm sure he'd been upfront with them. Some didn't mind being used in that way, hell, maybe they were using him.

I'd never been a user or let myself be used.

Maybe that was my problem, why my life was navy blue.

I was drawn in by him, a man my exact opposite. He was hundreds of miles away, not looking for a girlfriend, but just messaging him added color to my dreary world.

sophia

WE'D BEEN TALKING for a week now. We worked and messaged each other every moment we could, usually falling asleep in the middle of a conversation. I wanted to know everything about this man.

The manwhore title still fit him perfectly, but I'd learned he was more complex. Even passionate and romantic, but his heart had been destroyed, and I needed to know why.

Me: Can I ask you something? If you don't want to answer, I understand.

Kayden: Shoot.

Me: What happened in your relationships to make you swear them off forever?

I hit send and wished I could've erased the message before he read it.

Kayden: It's not an easy answer. I've been divorced for

a long time, and I finally fell in love again four years ago. We were like oil and water, and it ended horribly.

I wanted to believe in the fairy tale, but I didn't know many people who found it and stayed married. It seemed like everyone I knew was either single or going through a divorce.

Me: Twice and you're out?

Kayden: My ex-girlfriend, Lisa, ripped my heart out, and I don't think I could survive going through it again.

I knew the feeling, but it didn't stop me from still trying.

Me: Heartache can make you feel that way. You're too young to give up on it, though. And really, you can't stop love—sometimes, it just happens.

Kayden: Not if I have my way. I'm not looking for love, and I stay away from any situation where it's even a possibility.

Why was I bothered by his answer? I furrowed my brows and took a deep breath because I needed to get my shit together.

Me: I'm sorry. You've just picked the wrong ones. You shouldn't give up on love, just your taste in women.

Kayden: Maybe, but for now, it's easier for me. I work seven days a week and keep myself busy. I'm happier than I've been in years, Sophia.

Me: I don't believe it, but you can keep lying to yourself.

Kayden: Tell me about your past relationships or your current one.

I bit my lower lip, thinking of a way to sum up my love life. There wasn't much to tell, though. Although I only had one major heartache, even my single life had been as dull as my married one.

Me: They've all been passionless, an endless sea of navy blue.

Kayden: Can I ask you a couple questions? It only seems fair since you've been questioning me.

Palm meet forehead. He always answered my questions; how could I say no? I swallowed hard, trying to figure a way out of it, but nothing came to me. Hopefully, he kept the questions simple and short.

Me: Go ahead—fair's fair.

Kayden: Did they hold you every night and kiss you each day?

Me: No. Does a kiss good-bye count?

I didn't want to admit to the mediocrity in my love life, but I didn't have anything to lose either.

Kayden: There's problem number one. Do you like to be held?

Me: Yes, but guys just don't seem into it.

Kayden: Maybe the guys you've been with. I fucking love it. One thing I miss about not being in a relationship. Okay, so what about kissing? Why only a kiss good-bye? I mean, that's how you kiss a friend.

I tapped my thumbs against my phone, thinking of how to answer. I always wanted more, but the men in my life didn't. The lack of passion was why I kept my nose stuck in books.

Me: I love to kiss, just haven't found someone who brings me to my knees with a kiss. It's always too sloppy or too neat. I don't even try to kiss anymore, why be disappointed?

Kayden: Ahh... Maybe you're the problem. Maybe you're a bad kisser.

My mouth hung open. How dare he think I'm the problem? I typed faster, my anger at his statement making my fingers fly across the tiny screen keyboard.

Me: WTF. No! I'm a damn good kisser, or at least I used to be.

Kayden: I don't know about that. There has to be some reason behind it. I could tell you...if you're good or not.

The thought of kissing Kayden sent tingles throughout my body. *Do. Not. Geek. Out.* My fingers shook as I typed my reply.

Me: Oh, you're the authority?

Kayden: I've never had any complaints, and I'm just offering to help you out.

Me: You're so full of shit.

Kayden: The offer stands, Sophia. When you want me to give you my honest opinion, all you have to do is call me. My number is...

I quickly added his number to my contacts, not wanting to take any chance of losing it. He didn't ask for mine, but if he would've asked, I would've given it to him.

I don't know what it was about him that had me adding him to my contacts. Maybe someday I'd grow a pair of balls or get so bored, I'd take him up on his offer.

* * *

All-consuming.

It was the only phrase that accurately described my thoughts over the last three weeks. Kayden had taken up my every thought, my dreams, and my fantasies. I hadn't spent as much time with Gary since I started chatting with Kayden. My conversations, although I'd never heard his voice, were far more interesting than anything Gary had ever said or done.

Kayden: I want to hear your voice, Sophia. Can we talk instead? It's just hard for me to type right now.

My heart raced as my fingers hovered over the keys.

That would take whatever this was to an entirely new level. I wouldn't be able to hide my shock or laughter like I could via text. I gnawed on my jagged nail. *Did I want to talk to him?*

God, it would be such a letdown if his voice was like a squeak toy or he sounded like Kermit the Frog. The fantasy of the man behind they keyboard was probably way sexier than the reality.

Kayden: You still there?

Me: Yeah. Sorry. I got distracted there for a minute.

Kayden: Call me, then. I don't have your number, woman.

I stared at my phone and tried to slow my breathing to regain my composure. I hit send and closed my eyes.

"Hello." His voice was smooth and deep, almost a purr in my ear.

"Hi." Even though I tried to keep my voice even, it cracked.

"It's nice to finally put a voice to the words."

I paced around the room, needing to find something to do to get my mind off the fact that I was talking to him. Kayden, colorful Kayden, hot Kayden.

What the fuck was I doing? Breathe.

"I thought about not calling you," I admitted.

"Why?"

"I don't know. It's a big step. Besides, I hate my voice." I cringed because I knew I needed to stop pointing out my flaws.

"Oh, stop. Your voice is sexy."

Knowing that he liked my voice made my heart misfire, and I knew I was in trouble. I kept telling myself it wasn't true, but over the last few weeks, I've developed feelings for a man I never met.

"Tell me about your harem of women. I find it fascinating." I needed to switch the conversation to something that would probably make me realize he was an asshole.

"I'm getting bored with them. I think it's time for a change."

Did I want to know what he meant by that? I

UNTANGLE ME2egment>

mean, shit, I didn't want to think about him screwing some girl while I had a lovely dinner with Gary. "A change?"

"I have someone very specific in mind."

"Does she know?" I was torturing myself at this point.

"I'd have to ask her, but I'm pretty sure she does. She's a smart girl. She had to figure it out by now."

"Maybe you should tell her."

"Okay, hold on a sec."

Utter silence. I swore at myself under my breath. What a fucking idiot I'd been.

I heard a low chuckle. "I want you, Sophia. I don't want just any woman. I want to taste you." His voice was smooth as silk.

My breath hitched, and I closed my eyes as images of Kayden fucking me, bringing me to my knees with pleasure, made me squeeze my thighs together. I was in so much trouble.

 21

sophia

SUMMER VACATION HAD BEGUN weeks ago, and I had entirely too much time on my hands. Daydreaming about Kayden had almost become the only thing I wanted to do anymore.

Suzy, my roommate, and I spent our days at the pool, soaking in the sun while she read and I texted him. I'd moved in with her a few months ago and grown closer than we'd been before.

Kayden: What are you doing?

Me: Swimming with Suzy.

Kayden: Send me a picture. Ask Suzy to take it. I want to see your swimsuit.

No way would I send him a photo. I didn't even like the few kids in the pool seeing me in my swimsuit, let alone sending a photo that could never be erased to a total stranger.

Me: No way in hell—not going to happen, Kayden.

Kayden: Please.

"What are you shaking your head about?" Suzy asked, setting her book down on the table between our lounge chairs.

"Kayden. He wants me to send him a picture."

"What are you going to do?"

I shrugged. "Any ideas?"

Suzy looked around and stopped on the glass doors that lined the back of the pool clubhouse. "Oh, I have a fabulous idea. Use the glass doors and take a selfie."

Kayden: Humor me, please.

"You're a genius, Suzy." I jumped up from my lounge chair and headed for the clubhouse.

Kayden: Come on, just do it. For me, please.

Me: Gimme a minute. Stop begging.

I stared into the glass, checking my reflection, and realized Suzy was a fucking genius. The image was muddy and dark, but it would give him what he wanted while not giving him too much. I snapped a couple of them, picking just the right one before hitting send. I had the biggest smile on my face as I walked back to my chair, feeling mighty proud of myself. I could almost hear the curse words from here.

Kayden: Damn. It's blurry. Can you take another one?

Me: Are you zooming in?

Kayden: Hell yes, but it's hard to see. You did that on purpose!

Me: You asked for a picture, and I gave it to you.

I smirked, knowing how frustrated I'd just made him. I loved teasing him and the playfulness of our conversations.

Kayden: I'm not going to get another one, am I?

Me: Nope, that's all you're going to get.

Kayden: Why?

Me: I don't want you seeing everything. Pictures aren't always kind and can't be erased.

Kayden: Oh, come on, Sophia. You're perfect.

That statement right there was why I didn't want to send him one. Me in a swimsuit wasn't perfect. My body was flawed, and after lying in the sun for the last few hours, I was also verging on hot mess status.

Me: Where's my picture of you? Fair's fair.

I wanted to see naked. I almost salivated at the thought. I had a fantasy of him without clothes, moving over my body, in my body.

Kayden: I'm working and can't take one now. I'm all sweaty too.

Me: I want something, anything.

Kayden: Bossy... One second.

A picture of him in his work uniform, covered in sweat, standing near a lush garden of tropical plants filled my screen.

I was enthralled by his eyes—the green flecks of his irises matched the color of the leaves behind him. He was so freaking hot.

Kayden: Come see me. It's summer and you're off. Come here. Have some fun. Live a little!

Could I? I wanted to hop in the car right then and drive straight to New Orleans, but I didn't want to be another fuck—meaningless and disposable. But I was also done being navy blue.

Me: Feel like adding another notch to your bedpost?

My phone began to ring right after I hit send, and my heart leapt in my chest.

"Hey," I said, trying to play it cool.

"Sophia, you aren't a cheap whore. I've never thought of you in that way...ever."

I sighed, still unconvinced. "Kayden, I didn't mean to make you mad."

"You didn't make me mad at all, Sophia. I just want you to know how I feel, what I feel for you. For the first time in a long time, I look forward to waking up. I check my phone and message you before I even crawl out of bed."

My stomach filled with butterflies—a feeling Kayden often gave me. "It's the same for me, Kayden. I only want to make sure I don't become just another girl to you. I have to think about it."

"I don't want another notch in my bedpost. I want to spend time with you. I want to show you this amazing city. You could use a little fun in your life—wipe away that navy blue."

Navy blue... I'd stopped seeing Gary weeks ago. I couldn't pretend to be interested in him anymore. I'd rather be home talking with Kayden more than spending the night with Gary. My fantasies and

25

daydreams of Kayden were far better than anything Gary could deliver.

"I'll keep my hands to myself. I'll be a gentleman. Come on, just for a weekend."

"So, you don't want to have sex with me?" I covered my mouth, shocked that I actually had the nerve to ask him that.

"Fuck yes, I do," he said, causing my core to pulse. "I plan on it. You won't be able to resist me."

He was so full of himself, but it didn't mean his words were a lie.

"Well, it's nice to know your self-esteem is still intact."

"What's stopping you?"

What was stopping me? Fear, mostly. For weeks, I'd been trying to live outside my comfort zone but had failed miserably.

"I'm not used to sharing, Kayden. I've never slept with anyone who I haven't been in some sort of a relationship with, and I need to decide if it's something I can do."

"I haven't seen any other women since I started talking with you. I couldn't do it. You're all I think about, morning until night. I even dream about you."

"Oh," I whispered, realizing he felt the same as me. "I thought when you disappeared, sometimes for an hour, that you were with someone."

"Baby, I need way more than an hour. What kind of men have you been with?" He chuckled.

Jesus. I loved when he said such naughty shit to me. I wanted to believe him, I wanted to buy in to the fantasy, but I didn't know if I could. Everything was perfect just as it was, and if I went there and he sucked... If we were a disaster, I wouldn't even have our phone calls and texts left to look forward to anymore.

"I'll let you know."

"If you don't come here, I'm coming there."

"Okay. We'll see if you can find me first," I teased.

For a solid week, I thought about nothing else but spending time with Kayden. The positives outweighed the negatives. I couldn't deny the pull he had over me. I needed to act on my feelings or break off whatever this was because he was becoming a distraction to any possible happy future that might be waiting on me that didn't involve him.

My heart ached at the thought of him not being in my life. He'd become a fixture, a necessity to me like the air I breathed and consumed my days in such a short time.

Kayden: Well, since you can't seem to make up your mind, I came to you.

Me: What?

My stomach dropped.

Kayden: I told you last week, if you didn't come to me, then I'd come to you.

Me: You're lying. You aren't here.

I looked out my bedroom window, glancing in both directions, but I saw no one.

Me: I don't see you.

Kayden: Look out the front door.

Fuck, did he really know where I lived?

My legs shook as I walked toward the front door, gripping my cell phone tightly as I readied myself to come face-to-face with him.

Kayden: I'm kidding. Just thought I'd get your heart pounding.

I froze and didn't feel relieved, but saddened that he wasn't really here.

Me: You're such a dick.

Kayden: I'm not there now, but I do know where you live.

Me: No, you don't. What's my address?

My palms grew sweaty against the plastic of my phone as I read my address on the screen. My mouth dropped open.

Me: How?

Kayden: The chat shows where you are when you message me with your phone, kiddo.

Fuck. I never paid attention to the details in the chat window. I knew it said a city but never knew it showed an exact location. I tapped on his message, and I could see exactly where he was at that very moment.

Me: OMG. I never knew that. I always thought I was untraceable. I thought this was safe.

Kayden: Are you saying I'm dangerous, Sophia?

I laughed because I knew he wasn't dangerous to me physically, but he could break my heart.

Me: Nah. I don't think you would hurt me, but I think you would turn my world upside down. I've always steered clear of men like you.

Kayden: Maybe you've been with the wrong men.

Me: Who would be the right type of man? You?

I wanted Kayden to be the right type, but there was a problem. He didn't want a girlfriend. At least, that was what he said in the past, but that was before...

I shook my head, not letting myself believe we could have more.

Kayden: You need a little trouble in your life...some excitement. You've stayed safe too long, and what did it get you?

Me: Navy blue.

Kayden: Exactly. Time to add some other color, baby doll.

kayden

THE GREAT PICTURE SHOW

I NEEDED to get her to New Orleans. I was heading down to Bourbon Street with Tom to enjoy the best New Orleans had to offer and wanted to use it as a way to draw her here.

Sophia: I'll miss chatting with you tonight.

How could she think I could leave her behind? She still hadn't given me an answer on coming to New Orleans, even though I asked weeks ago. I'd tempt her with the sights of the city, the allure of its beauty as I walked around tonight, sending her photo after photo until she caved.

Me: I'm taking you with me.

Sophia: What do you mean?

Me: I want you to experience the city with me tonight.

Sophia: Really? You're going to give me a tour of the city?

Me: Yes. I want you to see the beauty and the fun. I

want you to want to come see me so you can see it all in person.

"Hey, Tom, can you take a picture of me?" I asked, handing my phone over before I jogged across the street.

I laughed as I posed in front of a very large DANGER sign spray-painted on a cement separator. It was perfect. Tom snapped the picture, and I asked him to take it again in case he fucked it up somehow.

I sent her the photo just as we climbed on to the streetcar.

Me: The start of the tour.

Sophia: Are you trying to tell me something?

I laughed because Sophia seemed to know how my mind worked. We seemed to get each other. For some odd reason, I felt like I'd know her my entire life.

Me: Me? Never.

Sophia: Where to next?

Me: Down to Bourbon Street. Ready?

I sent her pictures of the inside of the streetcar and the stops along the way. I couldn't even leave the house for an evening and not find a way to make her part of it. I needed to talk with her.

I told her I didn't want to get involved with anyone, but it was a lie. When I said the words when we first started talking, they were true. But as each day passed, I developed feelings for her. How fucked up was that? I hadn't even met her, and I felt a connection with her unlike any I had before.

Sophia: It's beautiful and so different.

I sent her a picture of a beautiful courtyard that was filled with flowers and tables, and a fountain stood in the center of the courtyard, flowing with water and glowing.

Me: I want to sit in this exact spot with you and sip on a drink.

Sophia: I'd rather be there with you than sitting on my couch right now.

Me: Look at this.

I spotted a few girls covered in body paint and no shirts. They were taking pictures with random men on the street for money and earning a hell of a lot. I snapped a photo from a distance and sent it to her.

Sophia: Wow. They have no shirts on, and that guy is basically grabbing her boob.

Me: Yep, women do it all the time here. It's normal.

Sophia: More pictures please but maybe less boobs.

Me: Gotcha.

Tom and I walked down into the heart of the French Quarter, and I captured as many images as I could to tell her the story of my night. Tom was very patient, understanding my goal of luring Sophia to New Orleans.

"So you really like this girl, huh?" Tom asked me as we waited in line for another drink.

"I do."

"Giving up on your arrangements, then?"

"Yeah, she makes me want more. If she's anything

in person like what she is like online, then I want her and no one else," I told him, and it didn't feel odd saying it out loud.

"Interesting, bro. She hot?"

"Wait. Let me show you." I tapped the screen a few times until a photo of her standing by the ocean appeared, the very first one of her that caught my eye. She was wearing a flowing black strapless top and shorts. Her long brown hair was blowing in the wind, and she was wearing sunglasses. I stared at her for a moment, smiling like an idiot. "Here's the first picture I ever saw of her."

"She's beautiful, Kayden. I love her hair," Tom said to me as he moved his face closer, trying to get a better look.

"Her hair caught my attention first. She's not only beautiful but smart as shit, dude."

"Is she going to come here?"

"I'm working on it. That's why I'm taking all these damn photos. She'd love it here," I told him while switching back to camera mode.

"You'll do it. You're a persistent bastard," Tom said, handing me a drink.

I wouldn't give up. I was never a quitter. I knew whatever this was between us was worth the work. Sophia was the type of girl who deserved to be courted, and I was working my ass off to maneuver my way under her skin.

sophia

I HELD my breath as I hit send. I finally caved. I didn't know if I was going crazy or was just so horny that all reasonable thought went right out the window.

Me: I've decided I'm going to come to New Orleans to see you.

Summer was slipping away, and so was my chance to meet him before I had to go back to work. When the school year began, everyone wanted to swap stories about their summer trips. As of this moment, the only place I'd been was the community pool. I wanted that great story, the excitement.

Kayden: Seriously?

Me: Let me know when you can get off work, and I'll be there.

"Hello," I said, picking up the phone on the first

ring. I'd expected him to call immediately when he finally realized I wasn't full of shit.

Deciding how long to stay in New Orleans wasn't easy. Most of the time, I set the first meeting to last a couple of hours or over a cup of coffee, but I agreed to a long weekend.

I'd have my own car and a means to exit the city—and his life—if it didn't work out, which put my mind a little bit at ease. I wanted to get to know him, and it would be nice to reminisce about home with someone who actually knew the places too.

"I can't believe you're really coming," he said.

It would be a long drive, and I wanted time to relax and enjoy myself before having to do it again to head back to Tampa. I hoped that the trip and our meeting wouldn't be a disaster.

Kayden had made it clear in our early conversations that he wasn't looking for a girlfriend—he was finished with relationships. He'd been burned by women too many times and wasn't eager for it to happen again. He wanted a physical relationship with someone but not an emotional connection or a girlfriend—although, I felt a shift in his attitude toward me. I was seeking excitement, and he promised just that.

"I told my brother that I'm coming to see you."

"What'd he say?"

My brother remembered him but made a few phone calls to check him out since it'd been fifteen years since they were in high school. If he gave me the all clear, I'd finally pull the trigger and head to New Orleans.

"He said he had a call to make and immediately hung up on me," I replied.

"Do you think he's calling some of my friends?"

"No doubt—knowing my brother, he's looking for any red flags."

"I have to tell you something." His voice had changed, and the playfulness had vanished.

"Okay," I said and scrunched up my face. Nothing good ever came after that statement.

"I was arrested a while ago, and I'm on probation right now."

I was more than a little stunned at the news. I didn't know what to say or think. He didn't seem like a criminal but a hardworking, kindhearted person...probation?

Should I run? Fuck.

I never invited trouble into my life, but this was Kayden, and even though he omitted the information, I still wanted to meet him. It's not like we were going to fall madly in love and become a couple.

"What happened?" I already knew my brother would find out and tell me, but I wanted to see what Kayden would say.

"Well...it's the reason my last relationship ended."

Weeks ago, I did a search on him, but I didn't find a damn thing. My supersleuth skills were seriously lacking if there was something to be found and I missed it.

"I won't look it up. What happened?" I asked, trying to sound convincing because I'd already started searching on my phone while he talked.

Kayden explained everything to me. His girlfriend threw him out after a night of drinking, and he went back to their place anyway. He lived there too and had for years. But after he went back for his work clothes, the alcohol he'd been drinking got the better of him, and he threw her clothes in the swimming pool out of anger. The police picked him up hours later and arrested him for trespassing and property damage. The rest was history, and now he was on probation until he paid her back for all of her ruined clothes.

I mean, I'd been there. Been so pissed I couldn't even see straight, let alone think coherently. I could understand how sometimes things went way beyond what we expected when alcohol factored into the equation. We'd all had an experience where we woke the next morning horrified by what we'd done the night before.

Did he have an anger problem? I hadn't seen a glimmer of anger in the time we'd spent talking or chatting online—he seemed so easygoing. My brother found no trace of it in his phone calls, and everyone said he was a nice guy. That night could've been a single event caused by drinking too much.

I had no right to judge anyone on his or her life

experiences. Life was a series of events that helped us become who we were meant to be.

"Are we still going to meet?" he asked in a sad voice.

My heart pounded. I responded quickly. "Yes." I sealed my fate. I needed passion, and he just might be the cure.

SIX

kayden

MELTED

I NEEDED a good girl in my life, and I wanted
somebody I could trust with my secrets and my heart.
Sophia hadn't been with many men, unlike the
women I'd been involved with in my past, and that
made her even more desirable. My judgment had been
off for most of my life, but I was finally on the right
path.

I worked all day as she drove to New Orleans. I
asked to leave early, so I could get home to shower and
clean the apartment. I lived with Tom, my coworker
and friend, and he wasn't known for his cleaning
skills.

I wanted everything to be perfect.

"Dude, I can't believe you convinced her to come
here for a weekend," Tom said, lying on the couch
watching television.

CHELLE BLISS

I nodded, feeling a little shocked myself. "She's fucking hot, man. She's unlike any other girl I know."

My phone rang, and I almost jumped out of the chair with excitement. She was here. I couldn't believe she was here.

"Hello," she said as soon as I answered. "I just got off the freeway, and I'll be there in a few minutes."

"I'll be outside waiting, Sophia."

"It's the moment of truth," Tom teased as soon as I hung up the phone. He didn't believe she could actually be as hot as she was in the photos.

"Fuck off," I told him before walking back into the bathroom to checked myself one last time in the mirror, taking a slug of mouthwash and swishing it quickly.

I ignored his comments as I made my way outside, not wanting to miss her pulling into the parking lot. I sat in my truck and watched the street, keeping an eye out for her. I could barely breathe as I waited. I didn't remember another time in my life that I was so excited and nervous that I felt like I could jump out of my own skin.

She pulled into the drive, and I caught my first glimpse of her. She was even more beautiful in person than I had imagined.

Would she still like me when she met me? God, I hoped so.

She looked around, zooming in on me, and smiled. Thank God! She must not be disappointed.

40

Seeing her made me realize I'd been a fool. I'd given up on love and a happy future. But it was still possible, and my heart wasn't dead, after all.

sophia

I COULDN'T BELIEVE I was doing it.

I was going to see Kayden—a man I'd talked to for months but had never met. Even though it went against everything I knew was right and safe, I agreed to drive across numerous states to finally meet him.

I thought my heart would explode before I got there, the pounding growing harder and faster with each passing mile. I tried to steady my breathing and concentrate on navigating the streets of New Orleans, but it was useless.

"Stay right and take Exit One, West Napoleon Avenue. Your destination is one mile ahead on your right," the GPS stated.

One mile?

I clutched the wheel, adjusting in my seat as my clothes clung to my body. God, I seriously needed a shower. Beads of sweat started to form near my temples as I tightened my grip, causing my knuckles to turn white.

Get it together, Sophia.

"Are you okay?" he asked, his voice coming through the speakers.

"I'm just trying to figure out where I'm going. There are so many buildings."

"I'll guide you, Soph."

I looked for him in between the masses of cars, but I saw no one. "Do you see my car?"

"You just passed my building. Do a U-turn and turn by the black gate."

"Shit." I wiped my forehead, realizing I was only moments away from seeing him in the flesh. I wanted to look my best. Well, at least as good as I could after two days of driving.

Stopping the car in the middle turning lane, I checked myself out in the rearview mirror. *Not too bad even though I'm a mess inside.*

I sat there for a moment and took a deep breath. "I'm coming now," I said, blotting my face before applying powder to smooth my complexion.

Calm down, he's just a guy.

I turned back toward him—the man I had thought about constantly for months.

"I see you."

I looked around, trying to catch a glimpse of him. I spotted a gorgeous man...Kayden. He was smiling at

43

me, and my belly flipped. I had seen him in pictures, but they didn't do him justice.

"I see you now, too. Be there in a second." I hit the end button, needing a minute to freak out in private.

You can do this. Calm the fuck down.

I tapped my index finger against the steering wheel as the gate to his apartment complex opened painfully slowly. He stood near an empty parking spot, waiting for me, and with each passing second, I grew more anxious.

As I pulled forward, I drank him in. His body was muscular and lean, covered in a pair of white, knee-length shorts and a blue T-shirt. His only visible hair at a distance was a goatee that framed his smile. As the space between us closed, I could see his bright sage eyes sparkling in the sunlight.

His smile had been a mystery to me, but now it made my breath catch in my throat. He didn't like to show his teeth because of a gap that was never fixed. It finally filled my vision, and it mesmerized me. The display made my heart melt. His teeth were imperfectly beautiful.

I parked my car in a haphazard fashion, not caring if I was in between the lines. My heart rate increased, and I clenched my hands into tight balls, closing my eyes before reaching for the door handle. I slid out, leaving the door open.

"Hi," he said as he reached for me. His heart was

pounding as fast as mine, as if they were speaking a secret language.

Thank God I'm not the only one nervous.

I buried my face in his neck, closed my eyes, and inhaled the sweet, masculine scent. He didn't wear cologne, but the scent was purely him.

He backed away, and before I could open my eyes, his soft lips glided across mine. The kiss turned more demanding as he sucked my lip into his mouth, and I moaned. After weeks of verbal foreplay, I finally had his body pressed against mine.

The passion was palpable as he gripped the back of my neck, tilting my head up to give him deeper access. I opened to him, and his tongue swept inside, exploring my mouth. The kiss conveyed all the longing and passion we felt toward each other. My knees grew weak as the realization hit me that I was here—kissing him.

Have I ever been kissed like this?

His lips pulled away from mine, and I swayed a bit. "Let's go inside," he said as he steadied me and slammed the car door. "We'll get your stuff later."

He snagged the keys from my hand, locked the car, and slid his hand into mine.

I followed behind him, taking in my surroundings as we wound through the garden courtyard that led to his apartment. The units were stacked three high, lined with wooden porches connecting the doorways.

Birds sang in the trees overhead as the sun cast shadows upon the ground.

Stopping in front of the door, he gave my hand a quick squeeze before turning the handle. "The guys are excited to meet you." He smiled.

Another man sat in the living room, watching television with his hand shoved down his pants like Al Bundy from *Married with Children*.

By the looks of it, a man had decorated the place because of the sparse, non-matching furniture and no decorations. It lacked the female touch and had only blank white walls.

"Tom, this is Sophia. Sophia, this is Tom," he said as we moved through the living room without stopping.

"Hey," Tom said, finally looking up from the television

My belly began to dance again, but I walked behind Kayden with confidence and a smile. "Hey." I waved to him as Kayden pulled me toward the hallway leading to his bedroom.

Unlike the rest of the place, his bedroom matched and had a completely male feel, filled with modern black furniture, a flat screen television, and a few simple decorations.

I turned around to face him, and his lips were on mine in a flash, guiding me backward. He kissed me deeply until the back of my knees hit the bed.

How far will I let him go?

I wasn't sure, not even in that moment, but my mind flooded with images of him naked, and I knew I wanted him.

He laid me on the bed and crawled on top of me, covering my body with his. Our hands moved across each other's bodies quickly, exploring every inch of flesh. The man could kiss, and it was intoxicating. We'd spent so much time talking, teasing, that the sexual tension was almost suffocating.

I'd lost all willpower due to his kiss, and his hands moved along my body, touching my breasts through my shirt and bra. I reached down, feeling his cock through his pants and gasped.

Shit. He was large. Bigger than any man I'd been with before and I knew this wasn't going be easy, but I wanted him just the same.

He chuckled, but he didn't stop as his lips blazed a trail of kisses down my neck, causing my body to break out in goose bumps. I wanted to feel his skin on mine, and I wasn't about to stop him from having his way with me. It had been so long since anyone had touched me.

He pulled my navy tank top down along with my bra, exposing my breast. His finger grazed my nipple, and pleasure shot through my body at the contact. When his mouth found my breast, I moaned and closed my eyes. *I wanted this...wanted him.*

His smooth hands slid up my thigh and into my shorts, pushing my panties aside. I rubbed his head and scratched his arms, unsure of how to react as he sucked my nipple harder.

Suddenly his head dipped down, and my stomach sank.

Was I ready for this?

He didn't attempt to unbutton my shorts as he kissed down my stomach before his mouth covered me. He licked and sucked like a starved man, and I freely offered myself up as a meal.

Pure ecstasy.

He stopped abruptly and moved back up my body, kissing me on my lips. "We need to go, Sophia. Are you ready to hit the town?"

"What?" One minute he was licking me in the most forbidden places, and now he wanted to leave?

I gaped at him, confused and achy.

He climbed off the bed and held out his hand to me. "We have to get out of here. If we don't, I won't be able to stop myself."

He's right. My body felt like it was at the point of no return, but I knew what he was saying was true. If we went any further, if I let him fuck me now, we'd probably never leave his apartment.

I rearranged my clothing and pulled my underwear back into place. "Okay," I said, but I felt rejected and it stung.

He helped me off the bed before I smoothed the wrinkles out of my clothes. I was at a loss for words as we walked out of the bedroom. In the heat of the moment, I'd forgotten about the guy sitting just a few feet away. My cheeks heated, and I started to sweat, feeling his eyes on me as we walked out the front door.

As soon as we stepped outside, Kayden placed his lips on my cheek, pulling me closer. "I can't wait to show you the beauty of New Orleans."

From this moment on, my life would never be the same.

My fate was sealed.

I thought I'd liked him before, but now...I knew it for sure.

Kayden Michaels had my heart.

DANGER WAS STARING me in the face—the same sign that Kayden sent in a photo during his tour of the city. My mind was consumed by a haze of lust and disbelief after what had just happened in his bedroom.

Kayden had had his mouth all over my body less than thirty minutes ago, and I didn't want it to end. I couldn't stop thinking about his rock-hard cock and the pleasure I felt from his mouth and large hands.

Kayden leaned against the wrought-iron fence separating the street from the streetcar platform, pulling me against his body, and my body complied with his not so subtle coaxing. My head lolled back and rested on his shoulder.

I couldn't stop staring at the sign, even though I knew it wasn't meant for me. Should I heed the warning? Kayden had already pushed me beyond my comfort zone within ten minutes of being in his presence. *Am I out of my league with this man?* My thoughts were interrupted when his lips brushed against my temple, and his thumb caressed my arm. The gesture was filled with love and adoration, and it took my breath away. I closed my eyes and became consumed in the feeling of his skin upon mine. I jumped when the streetcar whistle sounded to alert the waiting crowd of its nearness.

I turned my body, wrapped my arms around his neck, and stared into his eyes. I was mesmerized by the color and depth. The green center was trimmed in a brassy brown hue, resembling a turbulent ocean during a storm, and I was drowning in them.

"You told me your eyes were brown," he said, "but they're filled with gold and green flecks in the sunshine."

"No one has ever noticed that about my eyes before." I was in shock that he noticed the complexity in my eyes as I had with his.

"I want to know all of you...every spot on your body," he said.

I swallowed hard, and my mouth became dry as the words flowed through my ears and permeated my thoughts. I got lost in the possibilities that his statement held.

"Come on, babe. The streetcar is here," he said as he maneuvered my body toward the red and yellow streetcar.

The streetcar was crowded, but we found an open bench in the back. The wooden seats were small and caused every inch of our sides to touch. His hand rested on my knee as he turned his body to look out the window. As the car glided down the tracks, Kayden pointed out city landmarks and told me stories about the Big Easy. The street was lined with long and thin shotgun homes in all the colors of the rainbow. Beads leftover from Mardi Gras clung to the electrical lines like a jeweled necklace decorating Canal Street.

Kayden's touch never broke from my body. He touched every inch of my uncovered flesh as the car shook and lurched to our final destination—there was electricity between us. The car stopped abruptly and brought me back to reality.

"This is us," he said as he stood and held out his hand for me.

I rested my fingers in his palms as he helped me stand. He secured me under his arm as we started to walk down the busy street. The people of New Orleans were as colorful as the buildings.

"There's Bourbon Street," he said, pointing across the street.

My eyes followed his finger to a long, narrow street filled with people. I had heard about the decadence that can be found in New Orleans, but nothing prepared me for what awaited. My eyes grew wide as my feet touched the edge of Bourbon Street.

The street was lined with burlesque shows and

clubs, and girls stood in the doorways dressed in thongs and pasties. Their bodies convulsed rhythmically up and down the doorway, trying to tantalize the crowd to attend the show inside, and everyone was vying for business.

Kayden squeezed my hand as he studied my face.

"The whole street isn't like this. It changes to bars and restaurants before you enter the residential area. Hold my hand so you don't get lost in the crowd," he said. "Have you ever been in a strip club?"

"Not one with girls dancing, but I've gone to male ones."

"We're going to keep it that way," he said.

Music streamed through invisible speakers filling the hot, humid air. Bodies were swaying with the beat as they meandered down the street. The brick facades were lined with black iron balconies packed to capacity. The strip clubs gave way to vibrant bars packed with people.

"Want to get a drink?"

"I'd love something sweet."

"I've got just the thing. It's called a Hand Grenade, and it's a New Orleans specialty." He began to pull me down the street.

"What's in it?" I asked.

"It's a secret, but it's filled with a bunch of different things. It's sweet, but it's strong too."

A line of people formed near a small window to order a Hand Grenade to go. Kayden ordered one for each of us, and the bartender placed two giant green plastic drink glasses on the counter. The container was made of neon green plastic, and a grenade shape was at the bottom. I had seen many people on the streets carrying them as they walked. Kayden handed me the drink, and my first sip was an explosion of fruity flavor across my palate. I swallowed a few refreshing gulps before taking a breath.

"Slow down a bit. There's a lot of liquor in the drink," he stated as I removed the straw from my lips.

"It doesn't taste like there is any alcohol at all in it," I said.

"They're easy to drink and go down smooth. Have you eaten today?" he asked.

"I haven't had much to eat, and I'm hungry," I said.

"Let's get you something before you drink too much more," he said.

We sat on the stairs of the building next door and people watched while we finished our drinks. A drag queen directed traffic at the busy intersection, and the crowd followed his guidance, although some seemed confused. My legs began to tingle and feel like jelly. I needed to eat before I got drunk.

We crossed the street to Yo Mama's and entered the dimly lit doorway and went into the intimate dining room.

"There's an upstairs dining area. Let's go up there to eat for more privacy," he said.

The upstairs was furnished with tables and a separate bar area. All of the seats at the bar were empty, and Kayden picked two in the middle for us to sit.

"We can sit closer at the bar." Kayden pulled out a chair for me, and I collapsed into it. My chair began to move, and my body lurched to the side when it came to an abrupt stop. Kayden had moved my chair close enough to his that our bodies touched.

The bartender arrived a moment later to take our orders. Kayden ordered Jack and Coke, and I followed suit. My body was still vibrating from the nervousness and excitement of earlier in the day, and I thought one more drink would help calm me.

"Want to split a burger?" I asked Kayden. I didn't want to overeat, but I was starving.

"Sure, how about a burger and salad?"

"That would be fantastic. I'll eat any type of burger," I told him as I stroked his arm.

"It won't taste as good as you did. I can't get the memory of your taste out of my mind. I need another one."

"Later, Kayden," I said with a twinkle in my eye.

"Later? I want one now," he said as his hand moved up my thigh.

I flinched when his hand reached my shorts. He reached a finger inside my panties and found my wetness. He left it there for a moment while I looked around the restaurant to see who was near. No one seemed to be paying attention to us, but my heart began to pound. He removed his finger from my panties, bringing it to his lips. Smiling, he placed his finger in his mouth and sucked on it with closed eyes.

"Kiss me."

"What?" I asked.

He reached over and grabbed my neck to pull me close enough to kiss me. "I want you to taste yourself on my lips. I want you to know how sweet and delicious you are."

He kissed me deeply and passionately. I could taste myself on his lips and tongue. It was intertwined with his intoxicating taste that I craved more than any food. After a moment, he released me, and I sat there like a fool—unable to move.

I averted my attention from Kayden in order to gather my thoughts while he ordered our meal. I had never acted like this—public displays of affection weren't in my character. I clutched the cold drink and swirled the straw with my tongue. I had never felt such electricity with anyone like I felt with him.

"I'm dying to take you into the bathroom and fuck you right here. I won't, though. The first time needs to be intimate and last longer than a quickie against the bathroom wall," Kayden said in my ear in a slow, even tone. His words held promise of sexual pleasure like I had never experienced before.

I pretended to pout, although I could have never gone through with it. I had never had sex in a public place in my life, and the idea of it scared the shit out of me. Kayden made me want to do things outside of my norm. I wanted excitement, but would I be willing to do all it entailed? I didn't want a quick fuck in a bathroom either. I wanted it to be slow, so I could savor him.

We barely spoke while waiting for our dinner. We kissed and touched each other, and I couldn't keep my eyes off of him. I was drawn to his free spirit, and he oozed sexuality. His face was beautiful, and I couldn't stop gazing into his eyes. The food finally arrived, and we removed our hands from each other only to eat.

Kayden ordered another drink for each of us, and my stomach began to turn. The sweetness of the Jack and Coke wasn't harmonizing with all the other contents. I didn't complain even though I knew I would pay for it tomorrow. Kayden seemed unfazed by the alcohol coursing through his veins, unlike my jelly legs, hazy thoughts, and squinted eyes.

My stomach filled quickly due to the liquid floating inside. I watched him finish the burger and lick his fingers. His hands were large, and his fingers were thick. His lips were full and engulfed his fingers one by one. My thoughts were riveted by his motions, and I jumped when his hand trailed up the inside of my thigh. The people around us disappeared from my vision, and I was overcome with lust. The bartender was on her phone facing away from us, and he was driving me wild.

Kayden threw a fifty on the bar top and stood up. I

followed suit a moment later. My body swayed from the change in altitude.

"Steady," he said as his arms wrapped around my torso.

I giggled as he helped me down the stairs. The air in the French Quarter had become stale from the throngs of people. The sun had set while we'd enjoyed our meal, and the street was illuminated by neon signs.

"I could use a cup of coffee," I said.

We approached Café Du Monde, and a heavenly scent filled my nose, causing my mouth to water. The white building was decorated with a large green canopy to protect diners from the elements. The line stretched down the sidewalk, and we found a spot in the back. Kayden wrapped his arms around me and held me as we waited. His lips brushed against my ear as I stared at the stars twinkling above. I watched him place the order for me. I studied him: his smile, his body, and his joy. He radiated sexiness, and I wanted more of him, of it.

I sipped my coffee and swirled it around on my tongue. The taste was different than my normal brew, smoother and less bitter. We walked around the city until our coffee was finished and fatigue enveloped us. An illuminated sign filled my vision—The Funky Pirate.

"Would you like to sit down for a while?" he asked.

"Please."

The funky jazz music filled the air along with the stench of nicotine. Kayden held my hand as he walked through the bar and opened a set of wooden-slatted double doors. On the other side was a majestic courtyard. The courtyard was surrounded by brick walls lined with climbing vines entwined with beautiful white flowers. The ground was covered in bricks, tropical shrubs, and flowers. Lights twinkled above, held by a string, and they created a romantic atmosphere. The courtyard was empty, but the music flowed throughout.

Kayden ordered a round of drinks to cool us down after the long walk, and I didn't know if I could keep up with his ability to consume liquor. I put my legs over his, and he stroked my knee and thighs. We were alone, other than a trickle of people walking back and forth. It was romantic and sexy, but the alcohol was overcoming my ability to stay awake. I needed to sleep, and I wanted to be truly alone with Kayden. We walked toward the streetcar, and my legs wobbled as I walked. Kayden kept a firm grasp on my shoulder to help steady me.

The streetcar was standing room only. Kayden gripped the bar above his head with one hand and wrapped his arm around me with the other.

"Lean against me," he whispered in my ear.

I obeyed his request. I wouldn't have been able to stay upright without his help. The interior was dark, and murmurs filled the air. The trip went by in a blur, and I slipped on the step on the way out of the streetcar.

"Up we go," he said as he scooped me into his arms and carried me to his truck.

He propped me against the side of the truck, steadying me with one arm, while unlocking the door. He helped me inside and made sure I didn't hit my head by using his hand as a barrier. My eyes closed at the comfort of being seated in a quiet, dark place. It was so tranquil, and my body was so relaxed. The darkness consumed me.

"Sophia, we're back," he said as he touched my cheek to rouse me from my slumber.

"No," I said as I swatted his hand away.

"Come on, baby doll."

He opened my door and hoisted me into his arms. I wrapped my arms around his strong, lean shoulders and nuzzled my face into his neck. I inhaled deeply and almost tasted his scent. I could get lost in his scent and touch.

After he placed me on the bed, Kayden began to remove my sandals. I had been floating on a cloud until that moment. My mind snapped back into reality, and the brief sleep helped me regain my clarity. My eyes shot open, and all I could do was watch him undress me. The room was illuminated by candlelight, and the flickers danced on the walls.

"Is it okay that I'm doing this, Sophia?" Kayden asked, momentarily stopping all movement.

"It's perfect. Don't stop," I said with a giggle.

"Everything?" he asked, giving me a second chance to back out.

"Everything," I said firmly.

Kayden began to remove his shirt, and I watched in wonderment. I hadn't seen him without his clothes until that moment. His torso was long, lean, and covered in a smattering of dark hair. My eyes drifted from his chest to his taut abs and froze. He was unbuttoning his shorts, and I was riveted. He removed them slowly, and his cock sprang free as the shorts drifted to his feet.

"You're on the pill, right, baby?" he asked.

I swallowed hard, "Yes, and my last checkup was clean."

"Mine too. I was tested last month and hadn't been with anyone weeks before that," he said, crawling into bed.

A lump formed in my throat and my palms began to sweat. My heart was pounding so ferociously in my chest that it had to be audible. He threw my tank top off to the side, and it crumpled on the floor. I arched my back to give him access to unhook my bra, and it quickly followed the same path.

His lips trailed a path down my center to my shorts, and he paused. He glanced at me, asking for permission. I granted it with a smile. He undid the button with his teeth but kept his eyes glued to mine. He sat up on his knees and slowly shimmied them down my legs. Once my shorts were removed, I placed my legs wide enough for his body to fit snugly between. He climbed up my body and began to kiss me passionately as our hands explored each other's bodies. His skin was soft and warm, and I ran my fingertips over his back as he kissed me deeply, and we nibbled on each other's lips. His lips were full and smooth—and I couldn't get enough of them. I wanted to devour him.

The night had been filled with teasing and fore-play, and my pussy wept for him. He slid his fingers over my opening to check my readiness.

"I want to feel you, Sophia, skin against skin," he said in my ear.

"Yes," I moaned.

He stroked the head of his cock over my wetness. We had teased, kissed, and touched so much over the last seven hours that I was aching for him. I thought I was ready for him, but when he began to slide inside of me, I felt my body stretch painfully to adapt to the fullness. His cock impaled me, and I bit his shoulder to stop myself from crying out. His hips rocked slowly back and forth.

"You feel so fucking good," he said as he fully nestled his cock inside me.

I moaned in his ear as he withdrew his cock and slammed it back into my body. My back arched, and I was sore from the intrusion. I wrapped my legs around his back and hooked my feet together. The thrusts turned relentless and never-ending. My body was humming from the sensation of his cock moving inside of me. My body tensed, and he began to pick up speed. He pumped faster and harder until my body came undone. Flashes of light filled my eyes as my breath left me. I held his shoulder, unable to form a sound. The ripples of pleasure filled my world, and everything else ceased to exist. My body grew limp under his, and he tensed, his rhythm growing erratic. His breathing changed, and his eyes closed. I watched his face in wonder as he savored the same ecstasy that had filled my very being moments earlier.

No one had ever made love to me in the way Kayden had. My world had been altered permanently, and I knew that every man before him was a mediocre lover. He had ruined me for all other men.

He rested his forehead against mine and caught his breath. His lips swept across mine in a tender, loving gesture. His body fell to my side, and he put his arm above his head.

"I want to hold you," he said.

I immediately moved my body into the crook of his arm and wrapped my legs around his. I rested my arm on his chest and splayed my fingers in his goatee. I played with the hair on his face until I drifted into a peaceful sleep.

My stomach was doing flips, and my eyes popped open. The alcohol I consumed last night had made me queasy. I couldn't get comfortable. It was early, and we'd only slept a couple of hours. He opened his eyes and looked at me. I prayed he didn't regret anything and that he would still be the sweet man he had been the night before.

"Are you okay?" Kayden asked.

"I don't feel well. I don't usually drink so much. My stomach feels sick."

"What can I get you?" he asked me with a sympathetic look in his eyes.

I wasn't sure how to respond. I knew I needed something to help quell my stomach, but I was exhausted and wouldn't be able to sleep feeling like this.

"Maybe something to help my stomach feel better."

"Let me go see what we have. I know we have to have something around here," he said, stroking my face.

I watched as he crawled out of bed and headed for the door. His body was beautiful, and I still couldn't believe that I had sex with such a beautiful man. His ass was amazing—perfectly shaped and smooth. I didn't want to take my eyes off of him.

"Here, Soph, I found some medicine and some aspirin, so you don't end up with a headache," he said as he sat next to me on the bed, holding a glass of water and the pills.

I gulped it down, and he put the glass on the nightstand and crawled back under the covers with me. He grabbed me and pulled me close. I wrapped my body around him and curled up to drift back to sleep.

"I don't want to freak you out, but can I ask you something?"

Panicked, I put my hand over his mouth and said, "No."

What the hell was he going to ask me? I didn't know if I wanted to hear it.

My eyes were glued to him, and my hand remained over his mouth. I remained frozen for a moment until he began to laugh against my palm. I spread my fingers just enough to allow sound to pass through.

"Will you be my girlfriend, Sophia?"

Was this a joke? My mind went blank. Words escaped me.

"Your messages captured my heart, and I fell for you before I ever touched you. I didn't want to open my heart to anyone, but you, you seeped into my veins, bringing new meaning to my life. Being with you in person only made my feelings deeper for you, sealing my fate," he said. "I want you to be mine. I will not share you with anyone."

"Yes, Kayden," I said. His words stole my breath and warmed my body.

Contentment overcame me, and I drifted back to sleep tucked into his arms. I woke to the sound of rain thumping against the window panes. Kayden was sitting on the edge of the bed rubbing his eyes.

"I'll be right back," Kayden said to me as he picked up his shorts off the floor.

"I'm not going anywhere," I said to him as I sprawled out on his bed.

I heard the water turn on in the bathroom. I waited for him to return. I was too tired to do anything anyway. I heard noises coming from the kitchen as he moved around the apartment.

"Come on, baby doll. I ran a bath for us," he said to me as he pulled back the covers to reveal my flesh, his hands outstretched toward me.

I grabbed his hands and let him pull me out of bed. I followed behind him as he guided us to the bathroom. When I entered the bathroom, he had not only made a bubble bath but had candles flickering everywhere. It was romantic. No one had ever done anything like that for me before. I stopped in the doorway.

"What's wrong?" Kayden asked.

"You did this for me?" I asked, still in shock.

"Yes, for us. You don't like it?" he asked, concerned.

"Oh, I love it. No one has ever made a bath for me. It's sweet," I told him. I could feel my eyes filling with water.

"Well, get used to it. I want to take care of you. You deserve this, Sophia," he said to me as he pulled me toward the bathtub.

He stepped into the bathtub first, and I followed behind him. He sat down and helped me situate myself to be comfortable. I leaned against his body and felt totally and utterly happy.

"I know you don't feel well today, so no sex. This isn't just about sex for me," he said to me.

"No?"

"Well, not now, at least. I just want to lie here and enjoy being with you. Just relax." He ran his fingertips up and down my arms.

I relished and craved his touch. I leaned back, rested my head on his shoulder, and closed my eyes.

"I needed this. It's so relaxing," I said to him in a hushed tone.

"I am going to pamper you today and always, Sophia," he whispered next to my ear.

I was so relaxed I could barely speak. He continued to touch my skin softly and trickle water all over my body.

"I haven't been this happy in forever," Kayden said to me.

"You make me feel special—different—Kayden."

"You are. I've never known anyone like you. You make me look forward to each day, and I want you to feel the same," he said to me.

"I thought you didn't want another relationship?"

"I thought I was through with love, but that was before I met you. I can't imagine you not being in my life. I want you to be only mine," he told me while stroking my cheek.

"I'm glad I could open your heart again," I said to him as I stroked his legs.

I rested my head against his body and let the tranquility overcome me. He caressed and washed my entire body with a peach-scented soap. My senses were overwhelmed.

"Are you hungry?"

"A little bit. My stomach feels almost normal again," I replied while rubbing a hand over my belly.

"I'm going to make us something to eat. I want you to rest in bed while I cook," he said to me before kissing the back of my head.

Kayden helped me out of the bath and grabbed a towel. He slowly and methodically dried off my body, and my heart melted. He was so kind and gentle. After he was done, I walked back into the bedroom and crawled into bed. Kayden entered the room right after me and tucked me in like my father used to do when I was a kid.

"Rest a while. I'll be back in a bit to check on you." He kissed me on the lips. I watched as he disappeared into the hallway, and I closed my eyes and thought about Kayden.

"Sophia. Wake up, sleepyhead." I heard Kayden whispering while touching my face.

"I'm awake. Now."

"I'm making chicken soup, and it's simmering on the stove. I thought I would come pamper you a little more," he said to me as I sat up in the bed. "Can I brush your hair for you?"

"Really? You want to brush my hair?" I replied with wide eyes and a dopey grin.

"Yes, I love your hair," he stated matter-of-factly, walking toward my brush on the dresser.

"Knock yourself out," I said.

"Come here and sit in front of me," he said as he crawled onto the bed and patted a spot in front of him.

I did as I was told and sat in front of him. My hair was long and thick, and I hated brushing the tangled mess. He worked through each section of hair methodically and took his time. He made sure not to pull too hard or snag my hair. I sat there and reveled in the feeling of being pampered by him.

"All done," he said all too soon as he handed me the brush.

"Thank you. That was so relaxing. I've never had anyone, besides my mother, brush my hair," I said as I turned to face him.

"I'll do it for you, always," he said as he kissed me on the lips. I wanted to believe what he said was true. "I have to go check on the soup."

"I'm sure it's warm by now," I said, not wanting him to leave.

"Silly girl. I'm not reheating something from a can. I made it from scratch while you were sleeping," he said, shaking his head in disbelief.

"You made me homemade chicken noodle soup?" I

asked, still not believing he took the time and care in feeding me.

"I never eat soup from a can, gross. Stay here while I go check on it, and if it's ready, I'll bring you a bowl," he told me as he stood up.

I didn't want this dream to end. *Was I still asleep? Did this man really draw me a bath, brush my hair, and make me homemade soup?*

He walked back into the room with two mugs brimming with steaming liquid. The smell wafted from the doorway and reminded me of home. We stayed barricaded inside his room all day watching movies, snuggling, and enjoying his homemade soup.

Light filtered through my eyelids and woke me from my sleep. *Hot.* My body felt like I was sleeping next to a fire, but it was Kayden's naked body. I scooted away slowly just far enough to escape his heat. He was still fast asleep, and from my new position, I could watch him sleep. He slept peacefully, barely making a sound. He had a shadow on his face from his beard growing in, and his hand was tucked under his cheek. He looked almost childlike, unlike the wild sexual animal I knew was brewing under his cool façade.

His eyes fluttered open, and I quickly shut my eyes. I didn't want him to know I had been staring.

"Good morning, beautiful. I saw you looking at me," he said.

70

Busted. "I didn't want you to think I was a weirdo," I said as I opened my eyes and smiled at him.

"I already know you're a freak in the sheets. Why not add creepy sleep watcher to your resume," he laughed.

"I'm not creepy," I said as I smacked him playfully on his shoulder.

"What do you want to do today?" he asked while reaching out to move the hair away from my face.

"Can we go to the cemetery near the streetcar line and walk around?" I asked.

"That's different. I don't think I've ever been there with anyone before," he responded.

We left the apartment and headed to the cemetery. It was a hot day, and the air was thick with humidity. The sky was lined with puffy white clouds, and it looked like it might rain. The cemetery was empty—we had it all to ourselves. Kayden held my hand as we walked to the gravesites.

The gravesites weren't the typical headstones I was accustomed to. Small markers packed together row upon row, but they were unique buildings made of various types of stone. They were decorated with statues, stained glass, and iron gates. Multiple generations were buried inside the crypt-like structures. We peered through windows and entered the buildings that were open. While we were talking, the rain began to fall, but the sun continued to shine.

"Let's sit down for a bit and get out of the rain," I

said to him while pulling on his hand toward a building under a tree.

It was a beautiful building that was white with a green tinge around the edges. It was under a massive oak tree, and we found shelter from the rain. We sat on the steps with our knees touching, and he placed an arm around my shoulder.

"This place is beautiful," I said, noticing him watching me out of the corner of my eye.

"So are you, Sophia," he said as he brushed a piece of damp hair off my neck.

Goose bumps formed on my skin despite the steam rising from the concrete. He traced a line from the little strands of hair to my knee in one fluid move. My insides liquefied under his fingertips as I closed my eyes and exhaled slowly, trying to maintain my sanity.

The tranquility and beauty were awe-inspiring as the rain bounced off the leaves and formed puddles on the ground.

"It's strange that there's so much beauty in a place that is filled with sadness," he said to me as he stroked the back of my hand with his fingertips.

"It's so unlike anything we have back home," I said, trying to avert my eyes from him. The man still made me nervous in the most delightful way.

When the rain slowed, it became steamy outside—the rain never seemed to help cool down the air in the South. It only made it unbearable to breathe. Sweat began to trickle down my temples. The staleness of the air made it impossible to enjoy the serenity and beauty.

"Want to go back and cool off? I know I could use a shower before we go out tonight," he asked with a smile promising sin.

I gulped loud enough that I knew he had to hear, but he didn't let on if he did. Kayden climbed off the step slowly and held out his hand to me. I stood slowly while holding his hand and stared into his eyes. I tripped as I began to walk, and my heart plummeted as my face landed against his chest. Kayden reached out and caught me in his arms. I opened an eye and tried to catch a glimpse of his face as he pulled me away. I smiled as my cheeks began to heat, and I could feel the embarrassment spread throughout my body. Kayden smiled at me and grabbed my face lightly.

"We all fall sometimes in life, Sophia. It's more important how we recover," he said as he lips touched mine.

His thumbs stroked my cheeks while his fingers gripped the back of my neck. His kiss delved deeper as his tongue searched for mine. He possessed me. My mouth had grown dry from the heat, and his mouth refreshed me like an oasis in the desert. My body began to tremble with need. Emptiness filled me when his lips broke from mine.

"Let's go. I have plans for you, baby doll," he said with a wink.

* * *

My body hummed. Bourbon Street had led to another evening of excess. My legs wobbled as I walked down the streetcar steps. Kayden grabbed me by the waist as soon as my feet touched the street. I giggled as I tried to walk upright without swerving. My body didn't want to listen to my mind. Kayden placed my arm around his neck and kept a firm hold on me until we approached my SUV. Kayden opened the back door, and I stood there confused for a moment.

"In the back, Sophia. Now!" he said firmly while holding the door open for me.

I looked around, and only a trickle of people moved around on the streets at this hour.

He helped me as I climbed into the back, trying to avoid smacking my forehead on the door frame. The windows were tinted and gave us privacy. Kayden sat down and helped me place my body over his. My dress allowed him easy access as he pulled my panties to the side. A sheen of sweat began to form on my skin because the car was hot and the air inside stuffy. He unzipped his pants and guided his cock to my throbbing wet pussy. We had spent all night on Bourbon Street kissing and stroking each other—I wanted him.

I looked through the car windows on all sides and didn't see anyone. He rammed his cock inside of me, and all thought vanished. I no longer worried about the people on the street. We didn't make love—we had feverish sex in the back seat of my car. The only sound was our skin slapping against each other, our lips and tongues moving together, and our breaths fast and harsh.

I collapsed on top of him, exhaustion overwhelming me. We were breathing heavily, but he remained deep inside of me. He grabbed my thighs and held my body above his. He began to pump while holding my body in place. He increased speed and bit my neck, lost in passion. I cried out from the pleasure and pain. He invaded my entire being. My eyes rolled back in my head from the sensation of his cock thrusting in and out of me.

His thrusts began to slow until all movement stopped. Neither one of us climaxed, but I knew he was far from done for the night. I rested my forehead against his and tried to catch my breath. "Do you think anyone saw us?" I asked.

"I'm sure they saw the car rocking."

"What? The car wasn't moving," I replied in disbelief. I was horrified that someone might have seen the car moving.

"Oh, yes, it was. Someone had to see it moving if they were walking by," Kayden said with a sly grin and a hint of amusement in his voice. *Holy shit*. I had never been so reckless in all my life. Sex had always been in private. I worried too much about my career. Kayden had wiped all sanity from my mind and replaced it with only carnal intent.

kayden

I JUST FUCKED HER, but I needed more, wanted more of her.

"On the bed, Sophia. On your back, legs spread."

She crawled onto the bed in an unsexy way, but the spectacle made my cock grow harder. She was the sexiest woman I had ever seen, but she didn't know how to use it to her advantage. Thank fucking God for me. She flopped onto her back and lay there like a scared child, staring at the ceiling, avoiding eye contact with me.

"Wider," I said.

Her pussy was glistening, calling to me, an open invitation. I removed my clothes quickly before crawling onto the bed. My cock was throbbing for release, but I wanted to possess her.

I pressed my body against her but kept my cock out of reach of her dripping heat. I grabbed her breast and sucked her nipple roughly. I flicked it with my tongue and grazed it with my teeth. I moved my free hand slowly up her leg, skimming the tips of my fingers across her skin. Her body broke out in goose bumps, and her back arched from the difference in sensation. My fingertips reached the peak of her breast, and I pinched her nipple between my thumb and finger. I sucked and pinched each nipple in an alternating rhythm. Her hips moved as if in invitation, and her head dug harder into the pillow. I placed my hard cock next to her wetness. Her hips moved as if trying to swallow me, but I didn't accept the invitation. I wanted her to wait. I was in charge and wanted her to know it.

"Please, Kayden."

I climbed up her body and stared into her eyes. I rubbed my cock up and down through her stickiness as her eyes rolled back. I slowly glided the tip inside and could feel her pussy sucking and squeezing my cock greedily. My mouth closed over hers, and my tongue nudged her lips to open to me. As her body stopped demanding to be filled, I jammed my cock inside of her. She moaned into my mouth, and I withdrew fully from her core. Her hips arched from the loss of fullness, and a moment later, I thrust my cock to the hilt.

I lifted my upper body off and moved her hips, so I could sit back on my legs. I wanted to see myself buried inside of her. The candlelight twinkled off her skin and illuminated the fullness in her breasts. She was a vision, naked before me... Mine.

"What are you looking at?" she asked.

"I'm enjoying looking at your body. You're so fucking sexy."

"Stop looking at me and fuck me, Kayden. You're making me nervous."

"Nervous? I wish you could see my cock buried inside you. It's amazing. I want to enjoy you with my eyes before I feast with my body," I said.

She raised her arms and tried to cover her eyes with her arms. I slowly peeled them from her face, holding them by the wrists. I placed them above her head, gripped them in one hand, and pinned her to the bed.

"I will make you see yourself as I do, Sophia, if it's the last thing I do," I said. "I could never get enough of you."

She was at my mercy, restrained, and impaled by my cock. I began to move in a slow rhythm, in and out, wanting her to feel every ridge on my shaft. Her hips bucked as I increased the speed. I felt her contract around me like a vise. I reared up slightly and slid my hand around her throat. We'd spoken about sensual choking, and she was intrigued by the prospect but had never experienced it before now. Her eyes grew wide, but she didn't protest. I applied slight pressure on each side of her airway. Her face flushed, and her eyes closed slowly.

"Whose pussy is this?" I asked, moving close to her ear.

She didn't respond right away, so I stopped all movement.

"It's yours," she said.

"Whose is it? I can't hear you, Sophia," I whispered in her ear, once more waiting for her response before giving her the release she craved.

"Yours, Kayden. It's your pussy!"

"It is, and don't you forget it either. It's mine and only mine." I removed my cock and quickly slammed it back into her quivering core.

My movements became unrelenting and punishing, and I pressed a little harder on the veins in her neck. Her mouth opened in ecstasy as her hips moved off the bed. Her pussy began to milk my cock violently. Her body shuddered, moisture glistening across her skin. The contractions began to slow, and I released the pressure around her throat.

I chased my release, moving deeper and faster than I had before. Her body was limp and pliable under my grip. I gripped her ass, tipped her hips upward, and pounded her without guilt.

My cock grew harder, and my balls tightened. My body began to shake from the earthquake that was about to erupt from within. My world exploded as my vision blurred. The air in my lungs became trapped, and I was unable to breathe as my mind only had one goal...release.

I collapsed on top of her, unable to hold my body weight as my muscles weakened. I rested my forehead against hers and tried to steady my breathing. Rolling onto the mattress, careful not to crush her, I gathered her into my arms. Her legs entwined with mine, a sexy tangled mess of limbs and hair.

"I love being here with you," she said against my shoulder in a sleepy voice.

Her body stilled as I stroked her skin and played with her hair. She was asleep. Warmth overcame my body, mind, and soul. She was mine.

The clock read four a.m., but I couldn't sleep... I didn't want to sleep. She would be gone in a couple of hours. I'd tried so fucking hard to close my heart off to the possibility of heartbreak, but Sophia made it impossible to stay on course. Before she arrived, I knew I only wanted her in my life, but I never thought I'd ask her to be mine. I wanted her to be only mine and know that I was committed to her.

She slept so peacefully. I could watch her sleep for an eternity. My sole purpose for survival consisted of work and meaningless sex, but Sophia turned my world on its head. She was a bit shy compared to her online personality, but there was a sexuality that oozed from her timid demeanor. She'd always been a self-described bookworm, but I knew she had a wildness she had always suppressed, until me.

Fuck, she could ruin me.

I watched the minutes tick by, dreading the

moment my alarm would signal the end. Her eyes flew open as the alarm began to screech.

"Good morning, handsome."

"Morning, Sophia."

"Have you been up long?"

"Nah, just woke up a few minutes ago," I lied.

"I'm sad the weekend's over. I didn't want to sleep last night," she said.

"Me too. Fuck, I'll come see you as soon as I can."

"I know you will. Maybe we can Skype, so I can at least see your face each day."

"Hell yes. Maybe you'll see more than my face, remind you of what you're missing." I moved my eyebrows up and down for effect.

I couldn't take the sadness. I needed my lips to be entangled with hers during our last moments in bed together. I conveyed all the passion and longing I felt toward her in that kiss. My cock grew hard and ached to be inside her again, but I knew she was sore. She would feel me for days as it was. I ended the kiss slowly with a bite of her lip.

"I have to jump in the shower, baby doll."

"Okay, I'll pack my bags," she said while stretching, giving me a full view of her naked body. Did she know what she was doing to me?

I showered quickly, not wanting to miss a moment. My balls were aching to be inside her again. This distance bullshit was going to be torture. By the time I finished getting dressed, she was packed and ready. I helped her carry out her bags with a heavy heart.

I grabbed and kissed her, cradling her face in my hands. I could feel wetness touching my fingers as she wrapped her arms around my body. Neither of us wanted the weekend to end, but the real world awaited our return.

Sophia drove away.

Motherfucker.

I never thought it would be so hard to say good-bye to anyone ever again. I had made sure of that until she came into my life. I had so many regrets in my life. How would my life have been different if I would have met her years ago?

sophia

THE CHIRPING of my phone woke me from a dream.

Kayden: I dreamed of you last night... Shit, did I wake you?

Me: Yeah, but I don't mind. You're worth the lack of sleep.

I rubbed my eyes and tried to focus on the screen. My eyes were so blurry without my contacts, and the screen was blinding.

Me: Tell me about this dream.

Kayden: It was fucking fantastic. It was such a tease, though. I wish I didn't wake up. You were face down, ass up, and I was pounding you, balls deep.

My mouth suddenly felt dry. His words elicited visuals that caused all moisture in my body to pool elsewhere.

Me: Like doggy style?

Kayden: Not really. Your face and chest are on the bed with your ass sticking up in the air, back bent. I would be standing, holding your waist, with my knees bent. It's an entirely different angle compared to doggy style.

I was so fucking clueless when it came to sexual positions. I'd always been the queen of missionary. I switched to my browser, looking it up, but nothing really explained it to my satisfaction.

Me: Um, I may have to look that one up.

Kayden: It's so fucking sexy and makes for a great view for me. I love that about you, so innocent and inexperienced.

I was sure it was a novelty to him, but my inexperience could become boring over time. I chewed on my lip, thinking it could happen one day.

Me: Ugh, maybe a little too inexperienced for you.

Kayden: Never. I can mold you into anything I want. It's perfect.

Me: If you say so.

Kayden: The dream will give me something to think about all day. Gives me chills just thinking of doing that with you. Next time I see you...your face will be buried in the sheets.

Oh, hell!

My lovers had been so bland in their lovemaking. I always wanted more...hair-pulling, ass-smacking, rough sex filled with passion. I had always gone for the safe, boring lover who preferred missionary position in a bed instead of fucking in a car. Kayden filled a void that I had yearned for.

We messaged all day, naughty tidbits that we wanted to do to each other. I ached for him. I couldn't wait for him to finish work, so we could Skype. I wanted to see him and maybe give him a peep show. Since he had a dream about me, I'd give him the images to match. I wanted to drive the man insane with lust for me. He might've thought I was innocent, but I felt particularly naughty when it came to Kayden.

Suzy and I spent the day together. We cleaned while we danced around the house—anything to help the time pass. I told her all about Kayden and about our time together in New Orleans. She and I were very different, but our friendship worked somehow. She was younger and always filled with questions about love, relationships, and sex. We shared a love of reading, although her tastes were a bit tamer than mine.

She wanted to know everything about our relationship. She was so blunt with her questions, but I never minded someone who spoke from the heart with pure curiosity.

"Did he use a condom?" she asked.

"No, we've been tested, and I'm on the pill," I said, chomping on a cookie.

"I don't know if I could do it. I'd be too scared."

"I've never been pregnant, even when I was trying. I don't think I have to worry about it. I take the pill out of precaution, not out of necessity."

CHELLE BLISS

"Did you really have sex in a car?" she asked, noodles hanging from her mouth.

"Yes, I kind of got lost in the moment. I've never had sex in public before. Thank God it was dark."

"I can't wait to meet him, Sophia. He's the first man I've heard you gush about in a long time."

My phone chirped, and I looked at the screen, hoping it was Kayden.

Kayden: I'm home and logged on, ready?

I excused myself for a bit and headed to my room. I grabbed my iPad off the nightstand and plopped on the bed. I tapped on his picture to connect, and he accepted after one ring.

"Hey, baby," he said, lying on his bed shirtless.

"You're so sexy." I moved my face closer to get a better look.

"Checking me out?"

"No, I just don't have my contacts in," I said, laughing and squinting at the screen.

"Liar," he said.

"I have something to show you."

Suzy tapped on the door. "May I come in?" Suzy asked timidly.

"Sure, Suzy," I replied quickly and with a snicker.

She opened the door and walked to the foot of my bed. My iPad faced away from her, pointed directly at me. She didn't know we were video chatting. She started talking about a guy she met through an online dating service. He wanted her to come to his apart-

86

ment but told her he had no furniture except an air mattress. She wanted my opinion on whether she should meet him or not.

"Absolutely not. Don't even think about going there. You don't know him, and I don't like the idea that he doesn't even have furniture. He could kill you and be gone, without a trace, in sixty seconds," I told her. *What kind of creep would tell a girl he met online to meet him at his apartment...without any furniture?*

"She's right. Don't," Kayden stated firmly.

Suzy looked around the room. "Kayden?" she asked.

I looked down at the iPad and smiled at him. She started laughing.

"I certainly hope it wouldn't be anyone else," he said.

She moved around the bed and flopped down next to me. They began talking about the stranger online. She pointed out to us that we were strangers who met online. In a way, she had a point, but we had a commonality. I had placed calls about Kayden and felt safe after my brother said I had his blessing. We both told her that she needed to be careful about who she met and always to make sure it was in public. She was such a trusting and naïve person with a kind heart, always thinking the best of people. She wouldn't know a bad person or an unsafe situation until it was too late. I had to look out for her and guide her.

Suzy stayed only a few minutes, and Kayden and I started right where we left off before Suzy interrupted.

"What were you going to show me, baby doll?" Kayden asked while he stretched, watching in curiosity.

"Nothing important," I replied back even though it was a complete and utter lie.

"Can you wait a second? I have to take this call."

"Sure, go ahead, take your time."

While waiting for Kayden, I removed my bra and T-shirt. I thought I'd give him a surprise. I could hear muffled speech in the background. I heard his door close, and his footsteps along his bedroom floor before his face appeared. His eyes grew in size, and a smile crept across his face.

"Damn. I fucking love your tits. I want to touch them," Kayden said, moving closer to his screen.

"They've missed your touch, Kayden. They ache for you," I said as I swept my fingertips across them.

"Sophia, you're making me crazy," he said.

"Good, I want you to remember what's waiting for you. I don't want you to see any other women or even think of them," I replied to him, continuing to touch my breasts in full view of him. "Want to see more?"

"I don't think my heart could take it. I don't think of any other women. You are the only person in my mind—all day, every day," Kayden said with a very serious look on his face.

"Enough of this for now—you'll be touching them

soon enough, handsome," I said as I started to lift my top over my head, covering my breasts. It gave him one last glimpse as I slowly put my shirt back into place.

"You're driving me crazy. I better book my ticket before my cock explodes," Kayden muttered, shaking his head with amusement.

Skype made the distance bearable. It helped me deal with his absence, but it made me want to be with him even more.

kayden

DING.

I rolled over to see what Sophia said, but it wasn't her. It was Lisa. My heart sank. Lisa had become a thorn in my ass. The bitch knew exactly how to fuck with my life. She'd become a master manipulator toward the end of our relationship.

Lisa: I've missed you terribly, and I haven't heard from you in a long time. Where have you been?

I sat there deciding how to handle her. Even though she ruined my life, I had gone back to her for a short time. I was lonely, at rock bottom with no salvation in sight, when Lisa called me after my arrest. She wanted me back and convinced me that she still loved me.

I went against the court-ordered no-contact order and spoke to her. Of course, it was all in the past, but a part of my past I was ashamed of.

I was already living in New Orleans when Lisa called to say she missed me and regretted all that had transpired between us. I had nobody serious in my life but my regular girls, and Lisa knew I still harbored feelings for her, so she used that to her advantage.

I bought her a plane ticket to spend a weekend with me. I thought her feelings were sincere, but I soon learned I was just being used. The entire weekend her phone was turned off or placed face-down, so the screen was hidden from my view. I knew something wasn't right, but I put it out of my mind for a chance at happiness again. She asked for money to help pay her bills, and like a fool, I still believed she was there for me and not my money.

Me: Stop playing games. I fell for your shit once before. What do you want?

Lisa: Don't be shitty. I was cleaning and found something you may want.

The bitch always looked for leverage.

After Lisa returned home after visiting me in New Orleans, she turned into the same rotten bitch I had known she was. My despair had led me astray. She took the nice guy in me, chewed him up, and spit him out. The result was a callous-hearted person. But Sophia had been changing me, giving me faith in love again, and I felt Lisa wanted to rip it into a million pieces.

Me: You have nothing I want, Lisa.

Lisa: I have your grandmother's wedding ring. Want me to just pawn it?

Me: Fuck no! I need that back.

Lisa: I'll be in NOLA in a couple of days with some friends. Want to meet for a drink, and I'll bring it to you?

Motherfucking bitch.

I left Florida with nothing. I had a no-contact order and could never go back to get my things. I wanted something, anything that was mine. My grandmother's ring meant so much to me, and I wanted it back from her. But at what cost?

Me: I just want the ring, no drinks.

Lisa: If you want the ring, you'll have a drink with me. I'll call you when I'm on my way to Bourbon Street.

I couldn't tell Sophia about seeing Lisa. I'd have one drink with the bitch and only one drink. Any feelings of love I had for Lisa died during her last visit. I wanted nothing from her but the ring.

A few days later, Lisa texted me that she would be in the French Quarter on Friday around seven. We'd meet at the Cats Meow, but I had to come up with a lie for Sophia. She would be expecting me to Skype with her.

Me: Hey, baby doll. I'm going to meet a couple of the guys for a drink for an hour on my way home from work. Can we Skype a bit later tonight?

God! I fucking hated lying to Sophia. My stomach turned as I waited for her reply.

Sophia: No problem. Just text me when you're on your way home. I'll wait up for you.

Me: I will. I'll still have my phone if you want to text me or need me.

I arrived before Lisa and picked a spot at the bar. My goal was to get the ring and fucking jet. I ordered a shot and a beer while I was waiting. I needed a drink to calm my nerves. I wasn't nervous about Lisa. I felt like shit lying to Sophia. I downed the shot of tequila and sipped my beer as I saw Lisa walk through the door.

She looked beautiful, but I knew the devil that hid under the veneer. She walked toward me as I looked away and turned my attention back to my drink.

"You never change," Lisa said.

"Neither do you," I said without looking in her direction.

She sat down next to me and ordered a glass of wine. She touched my arm, and I recoiled as if it burned.

"What the fuck, Kayden?" she said due to my abrupt movement.

"Don't touch me, Lisa."

"You once loved my touch."

"I don't love you anymore. You've devastated me for a long time, but I'm on the right path again, no thanks to you," I said while looking her straight in the eye.

"What do you mean, you're on the right path?

You'll always love me, even if you can't admit it," she inquired with her eyes squinted to display her leeriness.

"I've found someone. She is kind and loving and nothing like you. I've moved on. I know you did way before your trip to see me months ago."

"A love like ours lasts forever. She may occupy your time for now, but you'll be back," she told me with a smirk on her face. "You always come back."

"Never! You've done enough damage to me, and I don't think I could survive another round," I responded. "Excuse me for a minute."

She was driving me crazy. I walked to the restroom and stood at the sink for a moment. I looked at myself in the mirror, not happy with the person staring back.

I shouldn't be here right now, alone with Lisa.

I lied to Sophia and felt like shit about it. I wanted to be different in this relationship, and I'd started it with lies and secrets.

I'm an asshole.

I splashed water on my face and dried off before looking in the mirror one last time. I needed to get the ring and get the fuck away from this bitch. I needed to see Sophia and be reminded that not all women were users and abusers. I reached into my pocket for my phone, but it was missing. *Fuck.* In my haste to get away from Lisa, I left it at the bar with her. That sneaky bitch always crept through my personal shit. I prayed she hadn't looked through my phone, but who was I kidding? I quickly returned to the table to see that my phone was still where I had left it. I picked it up and flipped through it, and everything seemed in order.

"I'm tired from working all day. Can I please just have the ring?"

"Sure. I'll be here a few days. Want to get together another night?" she asked, ignoring my question.

"No. I just came for the ring. I want no part of you," I said as I stood up and threw a twenty on the bar.

"Come on. I have many parts that you've always wanted." She grabbed her breasts.

"Just the ring. That's the only thing I want from you." I held out my hand, waiting for her to hand it over.

"Here, but if you change your mind, all you have to do is call." She placed the ring in my hand.

"I'll keep that in mind." I jammed the ring in my pocket, ready to get the hell out of there.

I didn't look back as I walked out.

She was my past, and I needed to get home to my future.

I WANTED to wait for Kayden before falling asleep. I needed to see his face and wanted to find out if he enjoyed his evening out with the guys. I heard the chirp from my phone and practically ran to grab it, but I didn't recognize the number sending me the text.

Unknown: Do you know where your boyfriend is?

What the fuck?

I ignored the message and continued washing my face and changing into my pajamas. It chirped again moments later. I glanced at my phone a little more warily this time.

Kayden: I'm on my way home. Call you in a bit.

I didn't respond to his text.

My head was swimming with thoughts.

Unknown: He was with me.

A picture popped up on my screen of Kayden with a female at a bar. They looked happy and were smiling.

There had to be a mistake. *Had he been lying to me this whole time? Was I just a fun fuck? Another girl to add to his list?*

I stared at the picture in shock. His arm was around her shoulders, their heads were touching, and her hand rested on his forearm.

I couldn't believe I'd been such a fool. He didn't want me for anything more than he originally stated. He didn't do relationships, only friends-with-benefits.

I never responded to the message.

I knew by the picture that it was Lisa. I'd seen a picture of her before. I seethed, and I felt like my heart was being torn into a million little pieces. Kayden had lied to me. Was this the first lie, or had everything been a lie? I didn't want to know the answer. I was done being a fool and a pawn.

Kayden: Logging in to Skype now. See you in a minute.

The last thing I wanted to do was see his face. I held my phone and switched back to the photo from Lisa. I climbed into bed, logged in to Skype on my iPad, and waited a moment before hitting the video button. I held the phone screen up to the camera.

"What the fuck?" Kayden asked.

I couldn't see his face, nor did I want to, but I knew he saw the image clearly.

"Fuck off. You're lying prick," I said, hitting disconnect before he could respond.

I can't believe I fell for him. I can't believe I was blinded by his charm, good looks, and the sex... Oh, the fucking sex.

Immediately the video tried to reconnect, but I hit cancel. I didn't want to see or talk to him. I was through with his lies.

My phone began to ring, but I resisted the urge to answer. I decided to turn my phone off and try to sleep.

The anger turned to sadness...sadness about what could have been and the hole left in my chest. Tears flowed down my cheeks like a swollen river after a storm. I buried my face in my pillow and sobbed.

How could I not know he was seeing other people?

I was falling in love with him, and I'd been delusional.

kayden

DAMAGE CONTROL

WHAT THE FUCK JUST HAPPENED?

Why had there been an old picture of Lisa and me filling the screen? None of this made sense. My heart felt like someone was trying to squeeze it until it burst. I could barely breathe.

I tried to reconnect the video call, but she wouldn't allow it. I called her phone, texted her, messaged her online, but she ignored me.

Panic set in. Sophia couldn't ignore me all night, could she?

I needed to explain. There had to be some misunderstanding. How did she get that picture of us? I looked through my phone again and saw nothing to clue me in. It had to be Lisa.

Me: What did you do, Lisa?

Lisa: What are you talking about?

Me: Don't play stupid with me. I know you sent some-thing to Sophia.

Lisa: I just let her know that you're mine.

Motherfucker.

Sophia knew I lied to her about the entire night, but she didn't know why. All she knew was that I lied. I shouldn't have told her about being such a manwhore when we first started chatting.

Me: Goddamn you! I'm not yours. Stay the fuck out of my life. Did you tell her that I was with you?

Lisa: Yes, you're MINE, and Sophia won't stand in my way.

All I could think about was explaining everything to Sophia, hoping she would forgive me. I had to get to her...had to hold her. I hopped in my car and headed east. On the way, I kept trying to reach her. I called a coworker to have him fill in for me for a couple of days. Physical exhaustion set in, but my need to see Sophia kept me awake.

I parked my car in front of her house and sat for a minute. How could I get in the house without Sophia knowing? If she wouldn't answer my calls, I had to find another way. *Suzy.* I grabbed my tablet and sent Suzy a message.

Me: Suzy, I'm here to surprise Sophia. Can you let me in so I can wake her up?

Suzy: Hell yes. She'll be so excited.

If she only fucking knew, excited was not the emotion that Sophia would be feeling. I still had my work clothes on as I stood at the door and waited for Suzy. I looked a mess. I hadn't slept or showered.

The door opened, and Suzy greeted me with a giant hug.

"Thanks, Suzy. I appreciate this. I wanted to surprise her," I whispered in her ear.

"It's so romantic, Kayden," Suzy said, hugging me tighter.

I walked down the hallway to Sophia's room and stood there a few seconds to calm my nerves. I opened the door as quietly as possible. The blankets were tangled around her body as she slept. The light was streaming in through the windows, illuminating her face, and I could see where the tears had dried on her cheeks. Her face was puffier than normal, and I knew I had caused her tears.

I sat on the bed beside her and touched her face, following the path of dried tears down to her neck. She stirred slightly but didn't wake. I leaned down and placed a light kiss on her lips. Her eyes flew open. She looked at me with wide eyes before speaking.

"What the fuck are you doing here?" she asked before pushing me away. She sat up quickly and covered her body with her blanket. I reached for her, but she moved away. "Don't touch me."

"Sophia, what happened? Why did I see an old picture on your phone?" I asked her.

"I know you were with her," she snipped.

"It's not what you think. Please let me explain," I begged.

"I don't need to hear more lies. I can't trust you, and I was a fool to ever think I could."

"That picture Lisa sent you was from last year. It wasn't from last night."

"I don't want to hear it. Just fucking leave. Get the hell out of my life," she said while staring down at her hands.

"You're going to listen to me and let me explain." I reached for her hands and placed mine over hers.

"She contacted me about my grandmother's ring. I left it behind when I was arrested. She knew I'd want it back. She wouldn't send it to me, but she was going to be in NOLA for a weekend trip. I met her to get the ring and nothing else," I explained.

"I sat at the bar and waited for her. She tried to touch me, and I wouldn't let her. I told her I was happy and had finally found someone. I told her I was with you. I had to get away from her for a minute and forgot my phone at the table. She must have looked through my phone and found your number. I came out of the bathroom and demanded the ring and left. I wasn't there more than thirty minutes total. I swear. I'm not seeing Lisa. I want only you... I love you, Sophia," I groveled.

"I was falling in love with you Kayden. I trusted you, and you ripped my heart out. How could you...

with that evil woman?" Sophia asked as tears began to flow from her eyes.

"I didn't. It's on my phone. Read the messages on my phone between her and me. You'll see I'm not lying to you about why I saw her. I didn't want you to freak out. I'm sorry I didn't tell you." I would not let her throw us away. I would fight for us... for her. I stood up and pulled my phone from my pocket. I flipped to the messages Lisa and I had exchanged. I held out the phone to Sophia.

"Read them, please. You'll see I'm not lying to you," I said as she snatched the phone from my hand.

I sat on the edge of the bed and just watched her. I prayed that once she read the conversation, she'd forgive me. She moved her fingers on the screen to read earlier messages that were sent between Lisa and me. She put the phone down in front of me.

"Why weren't you just honest with me? I would've understood," she said, wiping the tears off her cheek.

"I didn't know how you'd react. I didn't want to lose you," I explained, reaching out and wiping a tear trickling down her face. "I'm used to being with jealous women. I should have known better. I'm so sorry, Sophia."

"I'm not jealous. I don't like being lied to, and I don't know if I will ever fully trust you again," she replied, reaching out to touch my hand as it lingered on her face.

"Just try. You're the only one in my life. My heart is

filled by you. I don't think you realize how important you are to me. I'm in love with you." I laid it all out for her. I was not going to be coy with my feelings, and she needed to know how important she was to me.

She didn't respond to my words, and I needed her to feel the love I felt. I reached my arm out, and she didn't back away. I wrapped my hand around the back of her neck and pulled her close. I kissed her with all the love and passion she evoked in me. If she didn't believe my words, I wanted her to feel them through my kiss. I backed away and looked at her face. Her eyes were still closed. I watched as they fluttered open and looked at me with the softness I had seen before.

"I love you, too, Kayden. Don't hide things from me anymore," she asked.

"I promise not to lie to you again. I can't imagine my world without you," I told her while drawing her into an embrace.

She felt right in my arms. I was glad she couldn't see my face. There was so much about me that Sophia didn't know.

I hadn't lied to her before, but I hadn't been entirely forthcoming with my past.

I would share all the gory details when the time was right.

We needed to get through this moment before I could share my entire story.

sophia

AFTER READING the messages between Lisa and Kayden, I knew he told me the truth. I would try to trust him, but it would have to be earned over time.

Being so far away from each other wouldn't help ease my insecurities. Kayden drove all night to apologize and explain his actions to me. We were both exhausted from the last twelve hours.

"You want to shower?" I asked.

"Yes, but only if you'll take it with me."

I crawled off the bed and stood next to him, holding out my hand. We walked to the bathroom without breaking physical contact. I started the shower and sat on the edge of the tub while he undressed.

"How long will you be here?" I asked.

"I have to leave in the morning. I'll be back soon, though. I already booked my flight."

He helped me up and slowly removed my pajamas. He climbed into the shower first and held me as I entered. He washed my skin from head to toe, and it was as if he wiped away the pain and distrust from my being. When he was finished, I reciprocated the act, but I used my hands. I lathered the soap in my hands before placing them on his chest. I slowly rubbed my palms and fingers all over his body, working my way down to wash him clean. After we both rinsed the water from our bodies, Kayden grabbed a towel off the rack. He toweled my body off gently, making sure not to miss a spot, and wrapped the towel around me. He secured a towel around his waist before turning back to me.

Kayden gathered me in his arms, and I clasped my hands around his neck, resting my head on his shoulder. He laid me on the bed. I watched as he removed the towel from his body and dropped it to the floor. I reached for my towel to remove it, but he shook his head.

"Don't. I want to unwrap you," he said as he moved toward the bed.

I laid my hands near my sides- and waited for him. He sat next to me and peeled the cloth off my body slowly, as if savoring the moment.

"Make love to me, Kayden."

Kayden placed his body next to mine, leaning on one arm to keep his weight off of my body. He placed his hand on my neck with his thumb touching my face. He kissed me slowly and sucked my lower lip into his mouth. The only sound filling the room was our breath, shallow and rhythmic. His hand slid down my neck to my breast and squeezed before rolling my nipple between his fingers. I moaned into his mouth.

His lips broke from mine and followed a path down my neck to meet his fingers. His tongue laved at the tip, and he pinched it with his fingers. My hips moved on their own as if begging to be touched, and his hand left my breast to push them back down. He sucked my nipple into his mouth, grazing it with his teeth. He cupped my pussy with just the right amount of pressure to quell my ache.

Licking from my breast to my belly button, his tongue dipped inside as I squirmed. He chuckled at my reaction before continuing down my bare flesh. His tongue moved to the right as if to tease me and prolong what I needed—his tongue on my clit. He nudged my legs farther apart, and I did so willingly. He licked lightly across my lips before drawing my clit into his mouth. I fisted the sheets and curled my toes as he continued the ravenous pursuit of my orgasm. My body writhed from the pleasure as he sucked harder. His tongue flicked as the pressure increased. Every nerve ending in my body screamed for the release, and my skin became damp. My eyes began to blur, and then his mouth popped off my core. I whimpered from the loss.

"I want my cock in you when you come." He prodded my core with his hardness.

He rubbed the tip against my wetness to ready it for my aching core. I missed him and the pain-pleasure combination he was able to bring my body. He entered me slowly, making sure I felt every inch. Before inserting his cock entirely, he stopped and stared into my eyes.

"I've missed you," he said.

"I haven't felt whole without you." A tear trickled down my cheek.

He slammed the remaining portion inside, and I tensed for a split second...until my body stretched to accommodate his size. He moved in and out of me slowly. I could feel the head of his cock stroking the inside of my pussy. I arched my back to move with his body, needing the friction and wanting the release.

"I love you," he said softly in my ear.

"I love you, too," I replied, barely above a whisper.

I wrapped my legs around his back, linking my ankles together. I clawed at his back, trying not to break the skin. My skin dampened from the pleasure, and my muscles tightened with the closeness of my orgasm.

"Your body is mine, Sophia," he said, slamming his cock into me.

"Fuck... yes," I screamed.

My entire body froze and my breathing stopped.

Ecstasy permeated my being. He thrust quicker and deeper, leaning down sucking my lip into his mouth.

I lay there unable to move. His rhythm turned erratic as his release neared. He adjusted my leg up to my chest to allow him to go deeper. I ran my nails up the side of his body from his thighs to his rib cage. The extra sensation put him over the edge. His entire body went limp on top of me. His forehead rested against mine while he tried to steady his breathing.

We were both exhausted. I curled into Kayden. I hated the thought of sleeping when we had such little time together. He stroked my arm, but the pace became slower and sporadic. His breathing slowed and his hand stilled. He was asleep. I placed my hand upon his chest and closed my eyes hoping for peaceful dreams.

kayden

NIGHTMARES & FANTASIES

I WAS LYING on the beach with Sophia watching the sunset. My vision filled with all the brilliant colors of the rainbow. The clouds floated across the sky toward the setting sun. My world was finally peaceful.

"I could lie here forever with you, Sophia," I said, keeping my eyes on the changing scene before me.

I felt Sophia squeeze my hand. I could see her body out of the corner of my eye, but something seemed different.

"Who the fuck is Sophia?" a voice asked.

"Huh?" I looked over in horror. It wasn't Sophia. I broke out in a cold sweat, and my heart started to race.

"Who's Sophia?" Lisa asked.

My body shook violently as my eyes flew open.

Breathe. It wasn't real.

I looked over, and Sophia slept peacefully in my arms. I kissed her forehead and pulled her closer to me.

"Sophia," I whispered, trying not to startle her.

She moved slightly before her eyes opened. Her eyes were the color of the forest in fall—brown with flecks of hazel and gold. Her eyes were her best feature...besides her hair. The thought of her shutting me out again was unbearable to me, but the drive to gain her forgiveness was worth every hour and mile I traveled.

We left the bed only briefly to have lunch and grab a movie. I had such limited time with her, and I didn't want to share her with the world. We crawled back into bed and watched the movie. The characters in the movie were talking about their fantasies, and I wanted to be hers. I wanted to be the man of her dreams, and everything she had missed in her past relationships.

"What fantasies do you have?" I asked her while keeping her secured against me.

"I don't know," she responded. "Can we talk about it later?"

"I want to know now. I want to make your fantasies come true. Just share a couple with me, please," I said, not allowing her to change the subject.

I prodded her about the topic, and she opened up about all the things she'd missed in her sex life. She wanted a man to dominate her, to be woken in the middle of the night and fucked in an animalistic way. Her fantasies had never been realized, but I could change that. She wanted the sex to be playful and passionate. She was an avid reader. It opened her eyes to a world of possibilities she previously didn't know existed. I would give her one of her fantasies before I left.

I restarted the movie, but my mind wandered. I'd start small because of her lack of experience. I'd choked, whipped, spanked, bitten, licked, sucked, and fucked in every position and hole possible in my sexual past. Nothing was off-limits to me, and I was willing to make all of her dreams a reality. I wanted to push her beyond her boundaries but not scare her. I wanted her to understand all the possibilities I had to offer. I was lost in my thoughts when the movie ended.

"What do you want to do now?" she asked.

"I've got a couple ideas." I leaned over and began to kiss her. My hand wandered down to her breasts. They were sensitive—a simple touch, and she was mine, willing to do whatever I wanted.

"Stay there," I said as I jumped off the bed. I searched for something to tie her up. I wanted her unable to move or squirm away from me. I found some scarves and belts that would have to do.

"What are those for?" she asked with raised eyebrows.

"I'm going to make one of your fantasies a reality," I replied while approaching the bed.

She giggled like an innocent schoolgirl filled with nervous excitement. I removed the blankets and sheets from her body. I'd seen every inch of her body, but she was still shy. I started with her wrists, tying them tightly enough to keep her still but not cut off her circulation. She tugged on the restraints and realized she couldn't get out.

I grabbed her left ankle, pulling her down the bed, stretching her limbs before tying it. I repeated the process with her right ankle and made sure to tie it to the very last bar. I wanted her spread wide and at my mercy. I placed a pillow under her ass to allow better access.

I stood there for a moment, just looking at her. She was helpless, exactly how I wanted her.

"I won't blindfold you this time," I told her.

"Should I be worried?"

I didn't respond. I would take her worry away, replacing it with lust. I wanted to fill her mind with only thoughts of pleasure and want. I leaned over her body, placing my lips lightly on her nipple. Her back arched from the sensation but begged for me to suckle harder. I wouldn't give in to her unspoken demand. I had control.

I released my lips and slowly tongued her nipple. She sighed deeply, showing her frustration. I licked a path across her chest to repeat the torture. I sucked gently before grazing it with my teeth. Her hips moved in invitation, but I refused to comply. I moved my fingertips fluidly over her arm to create goose bumps across her flesh. I continued to glide my fingers down her side to her hips.

"Please," she said.

"Be patient. I'm in charge."

Before she could respond, I kissed her. My hand wandered down to her pussy. I slid my fingers over her pussy, checking her readiness. I started gently with one finger. I massaged her clit with my thumb as she moaned against my lips. I rocked my finger inside and rubbed a second against her wetness before inserting it. As I massaged her G-spot, her entire body flinched. She writhed in pleasure as I continued to assault her senses. I removed my fingers, and she whimpered from the emptiness. I granted her wish and quickly shoved two fingers inside. Her body reacted violently. I rubbed her clit to make the pleasure overcome the pain. I moved my fingers quickly while rubbing the spot that would bring her mind-numbing pleasure.

Her body became damp, and her breathing increased. She was close to an orgasm, but I wanted to prolong her release. I removed my thumb from her clit but continued the relentless pursuit of her G-spot. Her hips began to meet the thrust of my fingers, and her body tensed. At the right moment, I returned my thumb to make her have a full-body orgasm. She shook, and her breathing stopped. Her eyes rolled back. Her toes curled, and she went rigid from the pleasure.

"Oh my God," she said in whispered tone.

"I'm not done with you," I replied, reaching into her nightstand and grabbing her vibrator.

"I can't come again so quickly," she said with wide eyes, staring at the vibrator in my hand.

I didn't listen to her statement as I turned it on. I applied the vibrator to her already sensitive clit. Her body sank into the bed, trying to escape the sensation. I pursued her, not letting her get away. Sitting between her legs, I pushed my fingers into her again. She thrashed, but I didn't relent. Her breathing was erratic. I knew she was close. I pulled the vibrator away.

"No!" she spat out.

I leaned over, placing my mouth on her clit. I sucked, tongued, and licked her pussy with just the right amount of pressure to bring her close to climax. When her body began to tense, I moved away.

"Fucker," she said.

I smirked, knowing I had her on edge. She would probably claw my eyes out if given the chance. I placed the vibrator on her flesh. She was helpless and couldn't stop the onslaught of sensations. She tensed, and I increased the speed of my fingers then curled them inside her. Her orgasm was intense, and she moaned and wailed through it.

I untied her legs while she tried to slow her breathing, but I kept her hands restrained.

I folded her knees to her chest before thrusting my throbbing cock inside of her. I rammed into her with such speed that I knew she would fight me. I wanted the release...needed it. I moved her legs so that her ass was off of the pillows and her knees were almost at her shoulders. I placed my body weight on top of her to curl her up into a ball. I could feel every inch of her inside. I never slowed. I wanted her sore. She was mine. I pummeled her, and she made noises I never heard her make before. Her pussy clenched down on my cock, and I couldn't hold out any longer.

My world burst into a million colors, and my body shook with pleasure. I had never come so hard and long. The aftershocks were tremendous. I collapsed on top of her, trying to regain my composure. I had to release her wrists, but at the moment, I couldn't feel my muscles.

When I finally released her, I rubbed her wrists and kissed them. I knew they would be sore, along with her pussy. I had assaulted her in a primal way. I wrapped her in my arms on top of my chest. I wanted to know if it lived up to her fantasies. She didn't complain, except for me not allowing her to have an orgasm. She didn't like being denied, but she loved that I had control. This was only the beginning of the sexual world I'd show her.

I ran my fingers through her dampened hair as we spoke. I drifted off into a trancelike state. I was wiped out physically and emotionally from the past twenty-four hours, and I never wanted to leave her side.

SIXTEEN

sophia

THE SECOND COMING

I SAT at my desk staring out the window when the realization hit me—summer vacation was over. It had been a whirlwind unlike any I'd experienced before. My excitement had always revolved around the characters in my books, but Kayden changed that. No longer did my fantasy live within the pages of my favorite novels. I lived them.

"Hellooo..." a voice echoed.

I blinked a couple times, trying to break free from my haze. I turned my head to see Suzy standing there.

"Oh, I'm sorry. I didn't hear you walk in."

"I can tell. Daydreaming again?"

I laughed. She knew me so well. "Kind of. I was thinking about how much my life has changed."

"Ya think? You're living what most of us only read about. I'm envious of your sex life."

"I've played it safe for far too long. I'm ready to have my world rocked."

"Sounded like more than your world was rocked last time he was here," she howled.

"Were you eavesdropping?"

"Whore, I couldn't turn the TV up loud enough to drown out the noises coming from your room."

"Lucky for you, we're going away this weekend."

"Damn! I was hoping for an encore. That man's a beast."

"Shh. Someone might hear you," I said, glancing around the library through the glass window.

"Oh please. No one else is here. I'm going back to work. I just wanted to bother you a little," she said, walking toward the door with a small wave over her shoulder.

"Love ya, Suzy."

Me: You. Me. Airport. Car. Sex.

I placed my phone back on my desk and checked my emails, trying to get myself back into work mode.

Kayden: Fuck. I just got hard. Look what you do to me.

A photo of his rock-hard cock filled my screen. My mouth watered, and my pussy twitched at the thought of him inside me. The last two weeks Kayden made sure to keep constant contact with me. He never missed an evening video chat since Lisa tried to destroy us and I'd almost shut him out of my life entirely.

Kayden would be here in a few hours, but time

seemed to tick away slowly. I tried to keep my mind occupied. Teachers flowed in to gather their necessary supplies for the first day of school. Everyone shared stories of their summer adventures, but I kept mine simple. I traveled to New Orleans, met someone, and immersed myself in the culture. I left out my drunken escapades and car sex.

I had no doubt Suzy would be sharing tidbits with my coworkers in the coming weeks. She couldn't keep a secret and wanted to tell someone about my summer. She'd already shared my adventures with her mother. She never shared the information to make me look bad. She was just excited for me, and it brought hope to her love life.

Kayden: Jumping in the shower and heading to the airport.

I pictured him naked, lathering his body and shaving his head. He'd be here in a matter of hours.

Me: I'm counting the minutes until I can kiss you again.

Kayden: Kiss? I can't wait to shove my cock inside you. Be back in a few.

I ran home after work to get ready. I wanted to look sexy. After a day of working, I needed to shower and redo my makeup. I had one hour before I had to leave for the airport. I shaved my legs and groomed myself to his liking. He'd asked me not to wear underwear to the airport. Although I always wore them, this time, I would listen. I put on a cute short sundress, which was his favorite and gave easy access. I wanted to feel him inside me before we headed to the beach. It would be rush hour, and I was impatient. I gathered my bags for the weekend away and headed to my car.

When I arrived, I parked in a secluded location. I waited for him outside security.

Kayden: I'm here, be there in a few.

I was shaking—I'd never been so excited and nervous to see someone. I tried to steady my hands and calm my nerves. He came into view wearing a white T-shirt and white and gray shorts. He looked handsome, and I couldn't wait to touch him. We embraced, and I inhaled deeply. I didn't want to remove my arms from around his body. He kissed me with hunger. We needed to get out of this public place and into a more private setting.

We held hands as we left the airport and entered the parking garage. The walk seemed to take forever, and he chuckled when he saw where I had parked—he knew why I picked that isolated spot.

He opened the back door with a smirk. "In."

I crawled across the back seat, so he would have room to get in the car. He sat on the seat, and I straddled his legs. I kissed him with a longing I had never felt before. He kissed me back with as much passion and lust, running his fingers through my long brown hair. He reached down and unzipped his pants. His fingers trailed lightly up my inner thighs. I ached for him—wanted him in me. My wish was partially granted as his fingers slid easily inside me. I was ready for him.

He kissed my neck as his fingers worked in and out of me. He used his teeth to pull down the front of my dress to expose my breasts. He groaned before sucking my nipple into his mouth. I was moaning and squeezing his shoulders, but I needed more than his fingers inside of me—I needed his cock. As if reading my mind, he slid himself inside me. I didn't know if my body would ever get used to his size, not as long as we lived apart.

It was slow at first. I wanted to savor the feel of him. I moved my hips, grinding my body into his, and I took all of him that I could inside me. I had missed the intimacy. His head was tipped back, and he grabbed my hips, slowing my movement. My hair dripped with sweat, and it fell between us.

The air was thick and smelled of sex. His body shook as I slowed my movement. I buried my face in his neck and gasped for air. I planted a kiss on his neck and rested a moment. When I felt his body go lax, I climbed off him.

We both broke out into laughter when we caught sight of each other outside the car. Our faces were flushed, our clothing and skin dripping wet.

"Damn, I'm so hot! I thought I was going to pass out," I said, breathing like I'd just run a marathon.

"That was sexy as hell. I don't think I've come so quickly since I was a teenager."

CHELLE BLISS

I grabbed a drink out of a small cooler I packed before leaving. I cracked open an energy drink and took a sip.

"I see you planned ahead, dirty girl." He held out his hand, waiting for me to finish.

"I thought you'd be thirsty from the flight." I smiled and shrugged my shoulders.

"Liar." He grabbed the drink from my hand and emptied the contents.

We climbed inside and blasted the air as we drove to the hotel. We had a room reserved at the beach for the evening. The next day we were driving to his parents' home a couple of hours south.

The hotel was plain gray brick with colorful doors. It faced the beach and would be perfect for one night. He undressed, facing away from me, but I couldn't stop looking at him. I soaked in the sight of his naked flesh.

"I got something for you," Kayden said smoothly as he started to turn around slowly.

"What?"

My mouth dropped open. "When? Why?" I asked.

"I did it for you—to prove my love to you. There's no one else, Sophia. I'm yours forever."

I moved toward him, bending over to see his thigh better. Black ink spelled out my name in beautiful cursive lettering. I touched it, and he flinched.

"It's still a little tender."

"Sorry. Wow! I don't know what to say." I couldn't take my eyes off of it.

"You told me no one had ever put your name on their body. I wanted to be the first...and only."

I stood quickly, wrapping my arms around him. He declared his love and proved it in a permanent way. It wasn't marker that could be washed off. It was tattooed on his skin...for eternity. I had so many insecurities when it came to Kayden. His life had been filled with wildness, while mine was lived through books. I worried I wouldn't be enough for him, but this showed he was mine. It didn't scare me, even though it should. The tattoo wiped out the worry I had for our future, my future. He might be a little crazy and impulsive, but I loved that about him. When I had doubts about Kayden's love, I just needed to remember I was always with him.

He grabbed me and slammed my body against the wall. He nipped at my lips with just the right amount of tongue as if sensing my need. His taste was sweet. He pushed my dress to the floor and crushed my body with his. His fingers trailed over my skin, softly moving them up to my rib cage and then to my breasts. Goose bumps covered my body.

He turned me around, pushing my chest flat against the wall. He bit the back of my shoulders and licked up my neck to my ear.

"Fuck!" I moaned.

I wanted his cock inside me. His fingers found my

throbbing sex, slowly entering me. His other hand moved to my stomach before sliding to my breast. His fingers twisted slowly inside my pussy.

I felt his hands wrap around me then, grabbing my thighs. I yelped from the feeling of my feet lifting off the floor. Carrying me by my hips and thighs, he placed me on the bed facedown, hanging over the edge, and adjusted me to his desired position. I tried to lift my head to see, but he pushed my head into the mattress. I closed my eyes and suddenly felt his hot breath on my ass. I wanted him badly, and I wished he'd just fuck me already.

I moaned and pushed my ass higher in the air, hoping he would get the hint. He backed away and slapped my ass. He rubbed the head of his cock on my pussy as his other hand pushed down between my shoulder blades. I kept moving around. I couldn't lay still while he tormented me. He slapped my ass again.

I knew that I couldn't do anything to make it happen any faster than he wanted. I lay there, eyes closed, waiting. The tip of his cock entered me and stilled. When I turned my head to look at him, my lips were captured by his mouth. He thrust into me, smooth and quick, and I moaned in his mouth.

After each thrust, he pinched my nipples. He picked up the pace and pushed into me rapidly. I moaned and thrashed against the sheets. I moved my hands to find something to hold on to as my toes curled, and my mind went blank. My body stiffened, overwhelmed with the orgasm that slammed into me.

I didn't want him to stop, but I didn't know how much more I could take. His body tensed. His rhythm slowed, and his breathing intensified. He collapsed onto my back, and both of our bodies were slick with sweat. He held me tightly and kissed my shoulder and then my neck. I flipped over, wrapped my legs around him, and kissed him on the lips. My energy had evaporated, and the only craving left was sleep.

That evening, we went to dinner at a quaint little restaurant on the ocean. He convinced me to try foods I'd never tasted before. We shared our dinners, had beer, and enjoyed the music before deciding to walk the beach.

The sand still held the warmth from the sun. Sand filled the crevices of my feet as the waves crashed over top. The sun slowly lowered below the horizon as we talked about our dreams for the future.

"Are we going to survive this?" I asked.

"Survive what?"

"The long-distance thing. It's only going to get harder," I replied.

"We'll be okay, Sophia. It won't be like this forever."

"I can't leave before the end of the school year, which is over nine months away."

"We'll figure it out. Let's take it one step at a time. It'll all work out," he said.

"Want to walk down to the pier?"

"Sure," he replied, sensing my need to change the subject.

The pier was illuminated, and a large crowd had gathered, catching our attention. Local artists displayed their work along the railings. A small table had bracelets adorned with names. I wanted one with his name. I searched, finding one and grabbing it quickly. I needed something with his name to display on my body too. Kayden paid the artist and placed it on my wrist. Distant lightning danced across the sky.

He let go of my wrist, brushing the windswept hair out of my face. "Let's head back to the room."

"I want to lie in your arms until I fall asleep," I said.

He wrapped his arm around my shoulders, and I rested my head on his chest as we walked back to the room.

I had missed sleeping with him—the intimacy. Kayden threw his clothes on the floor before I had a chance to put my purse down. He turned on the TV and switched off the lamps. I undressed quickly and crawled under the covers with him. I felt at home at that moment, my body wrapped around his and my head on his chest, fingers playing with his chest hair. His hand stroked my back as my eyes began to close. I moved my hand to his face and toyed with his goatee, gently tugging on the tip.

I had been in a deep sleep, but my body was now

in motion. Kayden moved my legs, and I didn't bother to open my eyes or ask what he was doing. I could feel his hardness against my back. His fingertips brushed against my opening, and I was slick and ready. He grabbed my hip with one hand and was holding himself against me with the other. Pushing slowly inside of me, he held on to my hips. His chest rubbed against my back. He bit my neck as he moved an arm around my waist. I leaned my body back into his and arched to allow him to have easier access and a better angle. He fisted my hair and held me in place while he used me as a sex toy. He pumped inside of me like a well-oiled machine before coming to an abrupt stop. His cock stayed nestled inside of my body as he pulled me tightly against him. I drifted back to sleep and dreamed of Kayden.

kayden

DEVOTION

I KNOW I shocked and scared Sophia with my tattoo. It seemed through all of our chats that no one had ever done anything special for her.

I knew that was extreme and a bit crazy—a permanent act, but she needed to know how important she was to me. She questioned my faithfulness, and I felt this would help calm her worries. I knew she'd be mine, forever. I would make sure of it. I'd give her everything I had to make her want no one else. I'd do my best to love her like she had never been loved before.

I'd be lying if I didn't admit that I wanted to run into Lisa during our trip. I wanted her to see Sophia and her beauty. I wanted everyone to know Sophia was mine—especially Lisa. She tried to destroy us, but Sophia listened long enough to forgive me. Lisa had always been a controlling bitch, not overtly, but the cunning type. Her pussy blinded me to the venom spewing from her mouth for far too long. Her fangs pierced my skin but didn't leave a permanent scar on my heart.

Sophia brought my heart back to life. She radiated good girl but died to be naughty. It was more than just sex for me, though. I adored her and wanted to cherish her. She needed to know she wasn't just another woman to me. She was *the* woman. *Mine*. Always.

I shuffled out of bed, careful not to wake Sophia. I knew she loved coffee, so I wanted to find her the perfect cup. I stopped by the front desk to ask for their help. They gave me directions to a café nearby to accomplish my task. I needed to be quick, though. Sophia didn't always sleep in, and she would notice my absence when she began to stir.

The shop was around the corner, and the aroma filled the street. I ordered her a large caramel something or other. I had never been a coffee drinker, but I knew she liked her coffee sweet and light. I ordered a small for myself because the smell sucked me in, and I'd catch hell if I finished hers before getting back to the room.

I slowly opened the door, trying to avoid waking her, while balancing the two drinks in my hand. I could see her body wrapped in the sheets, holding a pillow tightly against her chest. I placed the cups on the nightstand and leaned over to kiss her lips. She kissed me back without opening her eyes.

"Morning, beautiful," I said, backing away.

"I woke up, and you were gone. Where'd you go?"

"I figured you'd need a fresh cup of coffee." My eyes watched as she began to stretch but quickly sat up when she heard the word coffee.

Her eyes darted around the room. "You went and got me coffee, really?"

"Yes, silly girl." I reached for the cup on the nightstand and handed it to her.

She cradled the cup in her hands, sniffing the tiny opening on the white lid. "It smells heavenly. Thank you, Kayden."

"We have a long drive ahead, and I thought you'd want one before we left."

"Fuck."

"What?" I asked.

"I'm so nervous to meet your parents. What if they don't like me?"

"They will adore you. My mom already thinks you're the best thing to happen to me," I told her.

"You've talked to your mom about me?" Her eyebrows rose.

"Yes, I couldn't wait to tell her about you. She was impressed you're a librarian. I told her everything."

"Everything?" Her eyes were almost popping out of their sockets.

"She's my best friend, and I share the good and the bad with her," I told her with a laugh.

"Oh my God, you didn't tell her about our sex life, did you?"

"Not all the details, but she knows if you're with me that you have a freaky side."

"Fuck. How can I look her in the eyes now?" she asked, covering her eyes.

"My mom's the least judgmental person I know, and she loves you already. Don't worry so much, Sophia. Not many women I've dated have actually met my mom. You're only the third, and one was my ex-wife."

She shook her head, not believing my words. I couldn't wait for her to meet my mom. I rarely introduced women to her. She worried enough without meeting the menagerie of women that strolled through my life. They weren't the type to bring home and introduce to the parents but the type to fuck and leave.

"Want to grab breakfast and sunbathe before we go?" I asked.

"Yes, as long as your parents don't mind us showing up later."

"Nah, we'll meet them at the club later. I'll text my mom and let her know."

Sophia grabbed some things from her bag and changed in the other room. I couldn't wait to see her in a swimsuit. She always covered her body. The bathroom door opened slowly.

"You ready?" she asked.

"I'm dying here. Come out."

A leg emerged from the open doorway, but I couldn't see the rest of her.

"Sophia, lemme see already."

"You're not going to be happy," she said, hidden from view.

She hopped from the doorway into the room, throwing her arms in the air playfully.

What the fuck is she wearing? The only skin visible was her shoulders, arms, and legs.

"That's not a bathing suit, babe. Turn around." She twirled in a circle as the skirt lifted, barely showing her ass.

"Yes, it is." She placed her hands on her hips, ready to argue.

"I'm buying you a real suit today. One that shows off that fucking knockout body you have underneath that thing."

"Fine, but when you're not around, I'm wearing this one."

"I wouldn't have it any other way. When I'm not around, wear this one all you want," I said.

Buying a new suit would be my first priority of the day. We found a small shop I had seen on my way to the café. Sophia needed something sexy. She ran her fingers across the suits as she walked by them.

"These are all so skimpy, Kayden."

"Exactly! I want to see that fucking sexy body glistening in the sun. I'll pick some out for you to try on."

I grabbed a couple suits with little triangle tops and side-tying bottoms. She wrinkled her nose as she watched me.

"Wear one for me, Sophia."

She went into the dressing room, and I could hear noises of disgust coming from inside.

"Lemme see each one," I said.

She opened the door with a look of displeasure, and my eyes lit up. She looked phenomenal. Her attitude in that moment gave me a glimpse inside this woman. I'd never have to worry about her being too flashy or showing too much skin. She was modest, and it made my cock hard.

sophia

MEET THE PARENTS

WE ARRIVED a little past five to a full parking lot. My stomach lurched at the thought of all the strangers inside. I always hated meeting new people in large groups. People would be studying me, judging me.

I held his hand as we waited to be buzzed in to the private club. I couldn't see inside due to the privacy glass on the door.

"Here we go," Kayden said, opening the door.

Dozens of pairs of eyes fell upon us as we walked through the door. People around the room called out his name as if seeing an old friend.

"I spent a lot of time here after I got in trouble," he said, pulling me through the crowd.

As we approached the table, people hurried to make room and grabbed extra chairs. A woman with short blond hair approached us with her arms outstretched. She gave him a hug, squeezing him hard, and kissed his cheek.

"Mom, this is Sophia."

I grabbed his arm, unsure if his mom would welcome me.

"I've heard so much about you, Sophia. I'm so happy my son has found such a wonderful person." She wrapped her arms around me in the biggest hug.

Kayden walked around the table, hugging and kissing the older women. Their faces lit up when he neared. The men shook his hand and welcomed him back. Kayden turned to face me.

"This is Sophia, everyone...my girlfriend," he said, smiling at me.

"We've heard so much about you," said one woman. *Lovely*.

"Sophia, this is my dad, Joe," Kayden said, holding on to his father's shoulder.

His dad reached for my hand, holding it tenderly, and kissed my cheek.

"It's a pleasure to meet you, Mr. Michaels."

"The pleasure is truly mine, Sophia," he said with a wink. A total flirt and I finally knew where Kayden learned his charm.

"I'm going to get us a drink. What do you want?"

"Whatever you're having is fine," I said.

His dad sat down and motioned for me to sit. Kayden and his mother walked to the bar and left me behind. The group around me began to chatter about

Kayden and how well he looked. They kept saying how happy he appeared.

I watched from a distance as he spoke to his mother. It had been months since they had seen one another. The joy emanated from her body as she touched his arm and spoke to him. The bartender placed our drinks on the bar, and they both stood there and finished their conversation before returning to the table. He sat down and pulled my chair close to him.

The conversation flowed easily. He knew them well and cared for these people. I listened to the discussions and heard the concern in their voices when asking him about his life. The group cared for him like he was a member of their family.

After a couple hours, we left and followed his parents to their home. Nervousness filled me at the thought of being alone with them. Would this become an interrogation? My stress was unnecessary. They were kind, warm, and welcoming. We sat outside on the lanai and talked. I mainly listened. Finally, I excused myself from the table, wishing everyone a goodnight and kissed Kayden on the lips. He stayed outside with his parents for a few minutes before joining me in the bedroom.

"Hey, baby," he said, entering the bedroom as I was undressing.

"Hi, love. Happy to see your mom?" I asked.

"I've missed her a lot, yes. It was great to see her

under happy circumstances for once," he said. "She really likes you and thinks you're good for me."

"I'm glad," I replied as I watched him walking around the bed, beginning to undress.

I observed him closely. He wanted our skin to touch when we slept, and I loved it. He crawled into bed, and I adjusted myself so I could nestle into his arms. He held me as he watched television, and I drifted off to sleep.

I woke early the next morning and made my way out of the bedroom in search of coffee. I didn't have the energy to fix my hair or put on makeup. I needed the caffeine to function. An empty cup sat on the counter, and a freshly brewed pot called my name. I poured myself a cup of coffee and opened the sliding door to the lanai.

I froze. *Goddamn it.*

"Good morning, Sophia," Joe said.

Shit. Maybe I should have at least brushed my hair. "Good morning. May I sit with you?" I asked.

"You don't have to ask. Sit down here. It's nice to have you both here," he said as he turned back toward the television.

We sipped our coffee and talked about sports. He was surprised by my knowledge of sports and love of football.

"I have to get ready for work. I'll see you guys later today, though," he said as he stood up and grabbed his empty cup.

"You will," I said, slurping the last drop at the bottom.

He chuckled, "There's more in the kitchen. Help yourself, kid."

"Thank you," I replied, needing the extra infusion.

I walked behind him, quietly closing the door. I filled my cup as strong arms wrapped around my waist.

"Morning, beautiful," Kayden purred in my ear.

"Morning," I said, stroking his hands.

"What do you want to do today?" Kayden asked me.

"Anything is fine with me." I turned around, kissed his lips, and inhaled deeply.

"Um, I haven't brushed my teeth yet. That's kind of gross."

"I didn't smell your breath, silly. I always feel the need to smell you. I can't fucking explain it. It's the damnedest thing." I shrugged my shoulder.

I sounded so creepy, but I loved his smell and couldn't get enough of it.

"You're a bigger freak than I thought," he laughed and smacked my ass as I walked out the door.

"How about we go to the store and then come back and cook some food?" he asked me with a smirk.

Kayden and I often went back and forth about who could cook the best. He cooked for me in New Orleans, but I had a few items in my arsenal that could not be beat. My meatballs were fantastic—he claimed his were better. This was the day we would finally put the matter to rest.

"Okay, I'm going to make my meatballs. Then you tell me if yours are better," I stated with a laugh. I knew I had this one in the bag.

"When you're done with your coffee, we'll go to the store and settle the matter," he said as he kissed me on the lips.

* * *

We walked the aisles, and I threw my ingredients into the cart. I wanted not only to impress him, but his parents too. He decided to make soup for everyone.

"You have strange ingredients for your meatballs," Kayden said as he stared down.

"You'll see," I said coyly.

We checked out and headed back to his parents. I was ready to work my magic. We had the house to ourselves. We both began chopping our vegetables, garlic, and onion. I mixed all of my ingredients for my meatballs. A quick sauce simmered to cook them in, the aroma filling the air. I took my time forming each ball perfectly and placing them in the sauce.

The moment of truth had arrived. I selected a meatball and put it on a plate for Kayden to taste. I watched as he cut into it and smelled it before placing it in his mouth. He chewed slowly and kept his eyes locked on mine.

"They're great, but mine are still better," he said as he licked his lips. He wasn't going to answer truthfully. He couldn't be the judge of this competition.

His mother walked in the door and greeted us with a smile.

"What are you two up to?" she asked as she sat on a barstool at the counter.

"We decided to cook. Sophia made meatballs, which she claims are the best, and I made soup. Would you like some?" he asked.

"Sure, I'd love to try both," she replied.

She sipped the soup and complimented him on how good it tasted. She was right. It was delicious. She cut the meatball and placed a piece in her mouth. She chewed, and Kayden and I glanced at each other and then at her. We waited for her response.

"These may be better than my meatballs," she said as she popped another sliver in her mouth.

I beamed with pride, turning to him with a grin.

"When do I get to taste yours, Kayden?" I asked.

"I'll never make mine for you. No way in hell," he said to me with a small pout.

"Aw, come on. You have to make them for me," I pleaded.

"No, Sophia. You win. Yours are great. Mine are bland in comparison," he said, wrapping his arms around me.

We were unsure of what to do while visiting his parents. He lived in this town for years with his ex-girlfriend, Lisa. The ex who had him arrested and the reason he was on probation. I didn't want to run into her during our visit.

That evening we returned to his parents' social club to spend time with them since we would be leaving the next morning, and he would be flying back to New Orleans. A band was playing music from decades ago, and the people moved around the dance floor with grace.

An older woman approached the table. She reached out and ran her fingers across his head. "Hey, Kayden, want to dance with this old woman?"

Kayden smiled and laughed, "Thanks, Edy, but I don't think my girlfriend would like that much."

"I would..." Something hard hit my leg under the table.

"That's all right, hot stuff. Maybe next time," she said, looking me over before turning around and leaving.

"Why'd you hit me?" I asked.

"I don't want to dance with her."

"I would've loved to see it. You would've made her night," I said.

"If I'm going to dance with anyone, it will be you."

"Not tonight and to this music. Someday, maybe," I said.

"Why? I want to dance and grind on you."

I began to fidget. "I've never been a good dancer."

"I'll teach you," he said.

Fuck. I hated dancing. I was the awkward person unsure of how to move my arms and legs. They always seemed to go in opposite directions.

We shared a pitcher of beer, and my eyes grew heavy. We said our good-byes and headed back to the house to go to sleep.

The next morning, his mother took us to breakfast. Afterward, a woman I didn't know stopped us outside and said, "Honey, you don't know how lucky you are. When my husband was alive, he looked at me exactly how he looks at you. He adores you."

Her words struck me in a profound way. I never analyzed how Kayden looked at me. His friends and family said he looked happier than he had in a long time. I guess I brought joy into his life, but he'd done the same for me. A breath of fresh hair, the fun I'd missed, Kayden represented everything I'd searched for in my life but hadn't found until now.

There were so many variables, so many things that could go wrong in this long-distance relationship. I worried he would meet another woman who lived close by and wouldn't want me anymore. If that happened, though, the whore would have to see my name running down his leg and be reminded of me if he strayed.

It was a long drive back to the airport. We planned to see each other in a few weeks, when he returned to Florida. He said it would be best if I dropped him at Departures instead of walking him in. Tears formed in my eyes at the thought of saying good-bye. I would probably turn into a crying mess if I went inside and dragged the good-bye out any longer.

The moment had arrived—he turned to me and kissed me with one hand on my cheek and the other on the back of my neck. I felt tears streaming down my cheeks and onto his fingers.

"Don't cry," he whispered on my lips.

"I'm trying not to. I can't help it. I'm going to miss you terribly," I said through my tears.

"I love you," he said as he placed his forehead against mine.

We sat there for a minute, neither of us wanting to move.

"I love you, too," I whispered against his lips.

He pulled away and reached for the door handle. I couldn't let that be last time I touched him or smelled him. I jumped out of the car, walking to the trunk. He grabbed his bags, placing them on the ground lightly, and turned to me. I instantly hugged him—clutched him like a lifeline. Maybe I should hold him hostage. He would have to be the one to walk away. I couldn't do it. He kissed me again with promises of a future, and I returned it with longing. A kiss could convey so many words without a sound.

I hated saying good-bye. Even more, I hated not knowing how long it would be before I'd see him again. Driving home, I felt lonely.

Kayden: I miss you already.

The tears were still streaming down my cheeks as I realized I would arrive home to an empty bedroom, and even sadder, an empty bed.

He boarded the plane before I pulled into the driveway. I went inside and tried to make myself busy until he called me. That evening ended just like the others had when we were apart. It made my room a little less lonely to see his face and hear his voice.

THAT NIGHT, I drifted off to sleep while Skyping with him, even though I tried to stay awake as long as possible. When I woke the next morning, I could see his face on the screen. I watched him for a couple minutes before his alarm blared and he stretched, rolling onto his back.

"Good morning, Kayden," I said. I wanted to wake up in his arms. I wanted to touch him.

He flinched, forgetting I was there. "Morning, baby. Sleep well?" he replied, stretching enough to cause the covers to slide down his body.

"I did."

"It's nice to wake up to your voice instead of just my alarm," Kayden said to me as he rubbed his eyes to clear his vision.

"I wish I could wake you with a kiss. I'd give

anything to rub your chest and stroke your arms," I said to him with a goofy smile on my face.

"I wish you'd wake me stroking something else, baby doll," he said with a chuckle.

He moved his legs, and the blankets no longer covered him at all, giving me a full view of his erection.

"Dreaming of me again, Kayden?" I asked, staring at him with wide eyes. I would never tire of his body.

"Always. I'd make love to you if you were here. I'd have you crawl on top of me, moving your body slowly. I'd want to feel every inch moving inside of you," he said as he reached down and began to touch himself.

"I want that—my body misses yours," I said to him.

"I'd suck on those beautiful nipples while you moved at a torturous pace on top of me. I'd make you beg me to move faster and harder. I love when you beg, Sophia," Kayden said with a sly grin.

"I love your form of torture," I replied with an innocent laugh.

"Okay, enough of that. I have to get ready for work. You're such a distraction but a fucking sexy one," he said as he sat up and covered his cock, shielding it from my view.

"You're such a tease. Go get ready and text me in a bit. I'm going to lie back down and finish what you started in my dreams," I said, blowing him a kiss.

"I will, baby doll. Catch you in a bit. I'm going to go

lather up and think of your fingers moving across my body," he said with a laugh, and then the screen went black.

I drifted back to sleep with thoughts of Kayden's beautiful body moving under mine.

* * *

I wanted to fill all of his senses while we were apart. I mailed him letters and small packages filled with tiny items to remind him of me. I wanted him to have something to look forward to each day. A couple contained cards or letters, perfume-scented tissue, his favorite candies, and things that made him smile. I never told him that I was sending them, and the waiting made me crazy.

Me: Are you home from work yet?

Kayden: Hold on... I'm busy smelling my Kleenex.

I smiled to myself. He was happy, and I was able to surprise him.

Me: What? Oh, you got one of the envelopes I sent you.

Kayden: Yes. I'm smiling ear to ear! You're the best!

He always seemed like such a tough ass, but I knew I could make him a pile of mush.

Me: Was it a puffy envelope or a regular one?

Kayden: I have more than one coming?

Me: Yes, a couple of envelopes are on the way... I spaced them out.

Kayden: Seriously? The card says it's about the little

things. Couldn't be more true. I opened the mailbox and had to look around because all I could smell was you.

I wanted there to be a constant reminder of me. I wanted my smell to be near, reminding him of my skin.

Me: I love that.

Kayden: Yes, whoosh... It hit me as soon as I opened the mailbox. I'm almost speechless. No one's ever been so thoughtful.

Me: No one's ever sent you a card?

Kayden: Birthday cards, but not one just to make me smile... It's all a double-edged sword.

He'd never had anyone treat him with as much thought and love as he always gave to them. I wanted to be different. I loved him. Everything about the relationship was a double-edged sword. I loved Kayden and wanted to be with him always, but the distance and our jobs wouldn't allow it.

Me: I know, love. I just wanted to make you smile.

Kayden: You did, incredibly large.

Me: It's a good day for you to get it. I know you had a shitty day at work.

Kayden: I love you so much.

My body grew warm and tingly. I could never get sick of seeing or hearing those words from Kayden.

Me: I love you, too. I want to make you smile every day. You work hard, and we are so far away. There will be more, mostly silly stuff. Now, stop smelling me. Get your shit done, so I can see you on Skype... I've waited all day.

Kayden: I'm going to put the Kleenex in my pillowcase. I want to smell you as I drift off to sleep.

I made sure to send as many packages and cards as possible. I wanted him to know that I was always thinking of him. I wanted him to know that he was loved and thought about...even if I couldn't be with him. he was always with me in my heart.

kayden

SOPHIA BROUGHT SO much joy into my life in such a short amount of time. I didn't want to do anything to lose her. I always seemed to find a way to fuck things up. There was still so much I needed to share with her, things she didn't know about my past. They were important details that made me into the person I was today. I had to find the right time to share everything with her, but would there ever be a perfect time?

She sent cards and packages a couple times a week. They gave me something to look forward to after a grueling workday. I filled my pillowcase with the Kleenex she sent me. I wanted to wrap myself in all things Sophia.

There were things I'd already shared with her that I regret. I never would have told her about the women I've fucked, the manner in which I handled those relationships, mostly my callousness when it came to love after having my heart broken so many times. I'd never thought we would meet, let alone fall in love with each other. She didn't seem to hold any of it against me. I was thankful she was so forgiving

She made me want to be a better man. I wanted her to be proud of me. I would be the man she deserved and always wanted. She was the most unique woman I have ever known. She had a knack for always making me laugh. Even on hard days, she found ways to make me laugh.

Me: Hey, beautiful. Can you send me a picture of the two of us?

Sophia: Sure, give me a second to find one on my phone.

Me: Thanks, baby doll. I want something to remind me of our time together. I have plenty of pictures of just you, but I want some of us.

She sent one from our first evening together, sitting on the steps of a building on Bourbon Street. We both wore goofy grins and had drinks in our hands. A smile crept across my lips remembering that evening.

Sophia: Here's one of us in the French Quarter.

Me: We have to take more next time we're together.

Sophia: Yes, I don't have a ton. We always get wrapped up in other things. We'll definitely take more next time.

Me: I need one to put on my nightstand.

Sophia: Just remind me, please. Time seems to go so fast.

The photo popped up on my screen. The glow of the streetlights bounced off my shiny head.

Me: Wow! My head is shiny in that picture.

Sophia: I love how smooth it is, and I love running my fingertips across it. It's why I have to wear my sunglasses all the time when I'm with you... The glare kills my eyes.

Me: Smartass.

I wanted to tickle her, bring her to tears.

Sophia: I read cataracts are caused by head glare, or is it sunshine?

Me: LMAO. Then you're totally fucked.

Sophia: I know because I plan to look at that shiny head for a lifetime.

Me: Most people would be insulted, but I know my head is fucking sexy.

I loved her most for her brains, her lightning-fast wit. I longed to be with her. I needed to book my ticket to Florida. I couldn't wait any longer.

sophia

MOTHER NATURE IS A BITCH

ME: *Have you watched the weather forecast at all today?*

 Kayden: I've heard people talking about a hurricane. Is it going to hit New Orleans? I thought it was going to make landfall in Texas.

 Me: They've changed the location. They're predicting NOLA now, and it's supposed to hit the day you're scheduled to fly out.

 Kayden: Fucking unbelievable! I swear I have a black cloud following me around.

 Me: You may have to postpone your trip.

I chewed my nails thinking about him being stuck in New Orleans during a hurricane. Would I know if he was okay? Visions of Hurricane Katrina filled my mind and made my stomach queasy.

 Kayden: I'm not staying in the city if a hurricane is coming. I'll see if I can cancel my ticket. If one is going to hit, they'll close down the office anyway.

Me: When will you know about work?

Kayden: By morning I'll know what's going on.

But the storm track never wavered. Landfall would be near New Orleans. Kayden canceled his airplane ticket, deciding to drive to get out of the path and to see me since all business had been shut down.

"I'm getting ready to leave now, babe."

"It's already five here. You worked all day, and it's a long drive. Are you going to be okay?" I asked.

"I'll be fine. I have a cooler filled with energy drinks, a bag of candy, and music to keep me awake. Knowing I'll be with you in a couple of hours will keep me awake."

"Just drive slowly, for God's sake. I'll be here waiting. No need to rush."

"I'll drive like I always do. I'll be there in about nine hours."

"That's what worries me. Be safe, love. I just want you in one piece," I said, sighing into the phone.

"I'll text you in a little while and keep you updated on where I am. I love you."

"I love you, too, Kayden." I tapped the end button on my phone.

I needed to keep myself busy while he drove. I knew he'd be careful, but the radar showed pockets of rain along the Gulf Coast, and it would be dark soon. I cleaned my bedroom, straightened up the house, and showered. His text messages were sparse, but each one gave me solace.

Kayden: I just crossed the Florida line and stopped for gas.

Me: Not much longer now. I'm tired. How are you going to stay awake?

Kayden: I'm wide awake, babe. Knowing you're my reward at the end keeps me awake. Lie down for a bit. I'll text you when I'm close.

Me: I'll set my alarm in case I fall asleep. I want to be awake when you get here, but I'm reading right now.

My eyes stung and grew heavy with each passing minute until I drifted off to sleep.

I blinked a few times to clear the haze that formed on my contacts as I grabbed my phone. *Fuck, my alarm never went off.*

Kayden: Forty miles away, paying a toll now.

Me: Which station?

Kayden: I have no idea. Just know I'm forty miles from you.

My heart pounded in my chest. I had to get out of bed. I wanted to be outside when he pulled in. I brushed my teeth, covered the dark circles that had formed under my eyes and headed outside, book in hand.

It was after one a.m., and stillness filled the air. The stars twinkled above as the moon illuminated my surroundings. Sitting on the front step, I opened my book, but I couldn't process the words.

A loud screeching echoed, and I turned my head to see what caused the vile noise as a white truck rounded the corner. My pulse went into overdrive as soon as I realized that Kayden was in that little white truck.

The truck came to an abrupt stop in the street and he jumped out, and I ran down the driveway. I jumped into his arms, unable to hold back my excitement.

His work uniform was dirty, his boots untied, and he smelled musky from a day of hard work in the sun.

"Surprised you, didn't I?" he asked.

"Yes," I said. A tear trickled down my cheek onto his shirt and relief flooded me knowing that he was safe.

"I'm gross from working all day, baby doll."

"I don't care. I'm just so happy you're here safely."

"I need a shower before we crawl into bed," he said, backing away from me.

"Let's get you cleaned up. You need rest," I said.

"One thing," he said.

His hands cupped my face as he kissed me. Not a passion-filled kiss, but one filled with love and relief.

His lips pulled away from mine. "Let me grab my stuff," he said.

He pulled a small bag from the passenger seat before holding my hand and walking inside with me.

I turned the shower on for him while he put his bag in my room, not wanting to waste a moment. While he showered, I undressed and crawled into bed. I heard the shower turn off, and my bedroom door opened. He crawled in next to me, and I instantly felt the warmth of his skin.

"I've missed you so much," I whispered to him as he hovered over my lips.

"I'm happy to be here with you," he replied and then kissed me passionately and with hunger.

"I love you, Kayden," I said to him as I melted into his arms.

"I love you, too. Sweet dreams, beautiful," Kayden said as he kissed the top of my head and stroked my arm lightly with his fingertips.

I woke before Kayden, as I often did. I watched him for a minute before I rolled over, trying not to wake him. I put my robe on and grabbed my glasses. I started the coffee and pulled all of the ingredients out of the refrigerator for breakfast. I wanted to surprise him, and I knew he'd be starving when he woke up.

Suzy emerged from her room when the scent of bacon and eggs drifted under her door. "Morning, Suzy," I said cheerfully as I continued to prepare breakfast.

"Kayden make it in okay? Although... I don't really even have to ask since you're so happy and cheerful this morning," she said with a chuckle, rubbing her eyes and stretching in the living room.

"Yeah, he finally made it in around one thirty," I said to her as I moved around the kitchen, prepping the toast and pouring the orange juice. "Would you like to have breakfast with us, Suz?"

CHELLE BLISS

"Really? That would be great. What do you want me to do to help?"

Suzy finished the eggs while I went to wake Kayden.

I opened the door and stood in the doorway for a moment. He slept peacefully, lying on his back with the blankets pulled up to his chin, holding a pillow in his arms. I sat down on the bed next to him and kissed his lips.

"Good morning, handsome," I said to him in a whisper just loud enough to wake him but not startle him. "Breakfast is ready."

"Morning, baby. I thought I was dreaming for a minute. I was scared to open my eyes and not be in your bed," he said as he reached out and stroked my cheek.

"I'm here, baby. Not dreaming this time," I said to him as I moved the covers off of his body to expose his naked flesh. "Come on, we can have breakfast before we decide what to do today."

He grabbed me, pulling me on top of him, and held me tightly against his hot flesh.

"Stop, Kayden. If we fool around now, Suzy will ruin the breakfast," I said to him while trying to get out of his grip.

"It's okay. Who needs food when I have you to eat?" Kayden said, kissing my neck.

"Oh, you're going to need your protein for what I've planned for you today, sweetie."

"Don't say another word. What are we waiting for?" Kayden said to me as he pushed me gently off his body and sat up.

"You're too easy. Promise of sex and you'll do anything," I said to him while trying to sit up.

"Only when it comes to you. I'm starving. I only ate junk food on the way here," he said as he rose from the bed and gave me a full view of his body. He reached into his bag and pulled out a pair of shorts. He opened the door, walked out, and left me behind.

I could hear him and Suzy chatting in the kitchen. Even though Kayden and Suzy had only spent a short period of time together in person, they both knew a lot about each other. Our time on Skype had helped us all form a bond. We sat at the table and talked. The chatter didn't stop during breakfast, and we all cleaned the kitchen together.

"What's on tap for you two today?" Suzy asked, placing the last plate in the dishwasher.

"Sophia said I needed my protein for whatever she has planned," Kayden said with a grin on his face.

"I'm keeping him locked up in my room all day. We aren't leaving the bed unless we need to eat. I want him to relax, and I want him all to myself," I said to Suzy while staring at Kayden.

"Well, have fun. I have a ton to do today," she said, walking into her room.

I had rented some movies before he left New

Orleans. He worked seven days a week and needed a couple days to recuperate.

"What do you have up your sleeve?" he asked me with a look of intrigue in his eyes, following me into the bedroom.

"I want to stay in bed and have you hold me all day. I rented some movies for us to watch. Oh, and make love, of course," I said to him as I stripped off my clothes and climbed into bed.

"Anything you want, baby doll," he said as he stripped off his shorts and crawled in next to me.

He made love to me, slowly grinding into me— face-to-face. I needed slow and sensual. It had been too long since I felt one with Kayden.

We both drifted in and out of sleep the rest of the day. He was like a tranquilizer; I couldn't stay awake snuggled in his arms.

The day was going too fast for me, but it always did when Kayden and I were together.

"Want to go grab something to eat?" I asked Kayden as I checked the time on my phone.

"Sure, I'd love a good cheeseburger," he said to me as he began to sit up.

"There's a place a couple of minutes away. They make great burgers," I said, crawling off the bed.

On the way to the restaurant, his phone began to ring.

"Shit, it's work. Should I answer it?" he asked.

"You better see what they want," I said, although I didn't mean a word of it.

"Hello," he said.

Kayden listened to the person on the other end before responding. "I just got here early this morning. Can't it wait a day?" His eyes darted to mine.

"Motherfucker," I muttered to myself turning my head to look out the window.

"But I had this weekend off before the storm," Kayden said.

"Fine," he said. "I'll leave in the morning."

He threw his phone down on the seat between his legs.

"I'm sorry, baby doll."

"You were supposed to have the whole weekend," I pouted.

"My boss said the storm has passed, and everyone is needed to make repairs." He ran his palm across his face. "He said he would make it up to me."

"It's fucking unbelievable. You just got here." Tears began to stream down my face.

"I don't have a choice. He said I have to come back," Kayden said. "At least we've had some time together."

"I know, but it doesn't make it any easier. I thought we had a couple more days together, at least. You drove so far to see me, and now you have to make the drive back already. I wanted you to have time to rest," I said to him while trying to get the tears to stop falling.

"Today has been great. It did more for me than you'll ever know. I promise I will be back as soon as I can. It may be three weeks, though, but first chance I get, I'll be on a plane to you," he said, trying to seem upbeat.

I couldn't do anything but think about him leaving so soon. The mood had been ruined. We barely spoke at the restaurant, and he tried to soothe me with loving touches. As soon as we returned home, I wrapped myself around his body and tried to crawl inside him. I could never be close enough, and this time tomorrow, he would be back in New Orleans. He made love to me that night, and tears streaked down my cheeks the entire time.

I slept horribly that night. Every time I woke up, I cried. My night had been restless and tortured. My eyes were puffy from tears, and I tried to prolong his departure. I didn't want to say good-bye.

When he drove away, I almost collapsed. When I knew he could no longer see me, I hunched over and sobbed. My tears fell onto the cement. To have him ripped from me in the blink of an eye was excruciating.

TWENTY-TWO

kayden

ABSENCE DOESN'T MAKE THE
HEART GROW FONDER

I DIDN'T WANT to leave her so soon. I knew in my heart I wouldn't be able to make it back for at least thirty days, but I prayed I was wrong. It depended on the amount of destruction the city sustained during the storm. I'd driven over eighteen hours during the last couple days to see Sophia. Every moment of the drive was worth even the little time I was able to spend with her.

When I entered the city, I could see the damage. Trees were knocked down, some neighborhoods had no electricity, street signs were blown away, and debris littered the roadways.

It could have been so much worse. The city was breathing a sigh of relief. Many anticipated the storm to be so much worse, especially since it was on the exact anniversary of Hurricane Katrina. I sent pictures to Sophia of everything I saw when I returned. We tried to Skype before we went to bed, but the internet connection was too sketchy due to the storm damage.

I sent her a photo the next morning on my way to work. I snapped one of me leaving my apartment with a smile on my face. I wanted her to think I was all right, even though I was a mess inside. I wanted to make her smile when she opened her eyes this morning.

When my phone dinged, I thought Sophia was awake and responding to my photo. I was wrong. Dead wrong.

It was Lisa.

Why couldn't she just leave me alone? There was a no-contact order in place between us. She was able to contact me all she wanted, but I wasn't supposed to respond. I ignored the message and went into my account and blocked her from sending further messages. I read her message before deleting it from my account.

Lisa: I saw your picture of your new girlfriend on your timeline. She's not your type.

What a fucking bitch. I didn't have a type. I loved them all. She must be watching me. Not a good sign for Sophia or me. She was destructive.

Lisa: Where's my money?

I wanted to reply to her, but I'd promised Sophia I'd ignore any message she sent to me. When I stopped for gas, I blocked her on my account. *Fuck her and her messages.* Lisa was my past. Sophia was my future.

* * *

Work kept me busy. I had to work the evening I returned home. The storm had damaged the city, but not in the way Katrina had years ago. Trees were down, and roofing shingles blown about. The levees held, and the city didn't flood. I immersed myself in my work, trying to keep my mind off the time I missed with Sophia.

My phone chimed while I was collecting my supplies for my next install. I threw the shit in the truck, unable to wait to see what Sophia had said. I pulled my phone out of my pocket and looked at the screen.

Tammy: You should know that I miss you.

Tammy? I'd never been with a Tammy. Never fucked or dated one.

Me: I don't know you.

Tammy: Not so much anymore.

Me: I know that saying. What do you want, Lisa?

She was persistent and sneaky. She had a fake account with a picture of a horse as the profile photo and a generic name. Unknowingly, I accepted her friend request a while back and never knew it.

Tammy: I want to stop thinking about you all the time. You should know that I miss you. I want you back.

Me: Look, we did what we did. But now I've found the perfect woman. Hopefully, you'll find your perfect man someday.

Tammy: I was always picking you up every time. Remember that, Kayden? I was always there for you. The past doesn't matter. I want you back in my life. I love you.

Me: You gave up on us long before I figured it out. You kicked me out and had me arrested. You fucked me in more ways than one.

Tammy: Can't we start over? I want you...only you.

Me: I don't want you, Lisa. I am in love with Sophia. Leave me alone, us alone. You tried to break us up once, and it didn't work. What's wrong, is your boyfriend not around? Is he not as passionate as I was?

Tammy: You always did know just what to say to make me remember who you really are. Passionate maybe, compassionate never.

Me: I should've never let you back into my life after having me arrested. You threw me out like a piece of trash. Can't have your cake and eat it too. I've always been nothing but honest with you.

Tammy: Never mind. It's sad that you're so mean now. Just remember, though, I love you and miss you.

Lisa destroyed me, and I'd been an active participant in the devastation. Even after everything the bitch had put me through, I still loved her afterward. That was, until Sophia came into my life.

I had to tell Sophia about Lisa's message. I didn't want to keep anything from her and risk losing the most precious thing in my life.

Me: Lisa is messaging me from a fake account. I'm sending you the screenshots.

I wanted to be honest with her, and she needed to know that Lisa was still trying to contact me and that the feelings weren't mutual. My phone rang.

"Hey, baby."

"Save the messages, Kayden," she said to me.

"Why?" I asked her with curiosity.

"You may need them later to prove that she's contacting you," she told me.

"She's allowed to contact me, but I'm not allowed to contact her in any way," I informed her.

"Do you still love her, Kayden?" Sophia asked me with a hint of sadness in her voice.

"I love only you, Sophia. My feelings for Lisa vanished long ago. She crushed any love I had for her. She's a sneaky bitch," I told her firmly.

"Okay. Just be careful what you say to her. Ignore her whenever possible. I couldn't deal with you going to jail."

"I won't. She would never turn me in for the messages she sent me. They aren't even from her account," I told her, hoping to calm her nerves.

I stored all the screenshots on my tablet. I had little hope they would be of any use, but Sophia asked me to do it.

sophia

CHANGE OF PLANS

FALL WAS IN FULL SWING, and I was excited for Halloween and all things fall. I was decorating the library for the students. There wasn't really a fall in Florida. The leaves didn't change, and the air didn't cool until well after Thanksgiving. I climbed off the ladder as I heard my phone chirp.

Kayden: I've been told to stop working. I just got a call from the main office.

Me: What? Why?

Kayden: They said there was an issue with my drug test or background check. I didn't really understand. It's bullshit. Let me call some of the guys and see what's up. BRB.

Nothing had changed since his employment with the company began. His past was finally coming back to haunt him, even though it had been a year and a half since the incident with Lisa. There had to be some mistake or a mix-up with the paperwork.

Kayden: Okay. Five other people were pulled off the job too. Headquarters came in, did an audit, and found an error in my file. I'm fucked, Sophia. I was told they're cracking down on background check results and their guidelines. I may not have a job anymore. Fuck.

Me: There must be a mistake. They'll straighten it out. Don't panic yet.

I felt ill at the thought of his world unraveling.

Kayden: I don't know what I'll do without work. I need to make some more calls and grab dinner. I'll call you when I get home, okay?

Me: Yes, love. Take your time.

Sitting on my bed, I chewed my nails, staring at the wall.

What the fuck is he going to do? Where would he go? He lived in company housing, after all. Would they kick him out? The thoughts swirling through my mind only heightened my anxiety. I needed to release some stress and decided to go for a run. Kayden called me hours later.

"Hey," I said answering the phone.

"Hi, baby doll. I'm making dinner and talking to Tom." I could hear a chopping noise in the background and Tom's loud voice. "I'll text you around nine to Skype. We're talking about work, trying to figure out what the fuck is going on. Is that okay?"

I wrinkled my nose, annoyed that I was being brushed off. "Yes, don't forget about me."

"Babe, how could I ever forget about you? We're

just having a couple drinks and bullshitting. I'll text, promise."

"I love you, Kayden," I said, wishing I could touch him at that moment.

"I love you, too, baby doll. Talk in a bit." The line went dead.

I tried to keep myself busy reading books and watching television, but nothing took my mind off Kayden. He hadn't sent me a message in hours. I flipped my phone in my hand, debating sending him a text first, but I couldn't resist any longer.

Me: Hey, it's almost nine. Are we going to Skype tonight, lover?

Nothing. What the fuck? Kayden had never ignored me. I texted him again, pacing around the room panicking. Silence.

Maybe his cell phone battery died. I sent a message to his tablet. I called his phone, letting it ring over ten times since he didn't have voice mail. No answer. My heart sank. What happened to him? We hadn't missed an evening since we met. He never disappeared. I felt lost and helpless with the distance between us.

My anger started to grow, and I needed to calm my nerves. Where was he? Who was he with? I couldn't let my mind wander and question his faithfulness. Why did I have to be so insecure when it came to Kayden?

I mixed some vodka with whatever else I could find in the fridge, anything to make it slide down easier. I'd never been a drinker, but I needed to take the edge off. I swigged a mouthful of the fruity concoction, closed my eyes, and swallowed. The liquid slid down my throat, warming my body from the inside.

"Hey." I jumped, startled by Suzy's voice.

"Jesus, you scared the shit out of me," I said, almost choking on my drink.

"What's wrong?" she asked.

"Kayden... He may have lost his job," I said, taking another sip of my drink. "We were supposed to Skype tonight, but he's disappeared."

"Wait. What? He lost his job?"

"I just don't know anything right now. I can't get in touch with him. I'm going crazy, Suzy." Suzy sat at the counter and watched me. "He was talking with the guys and making dinner last time I heard from him. That was over three hours ago."

"I'm sure he'll call you, Sophia. Kayden adores you. Don't freak out...yet." She tried to console me.

Her words didn't help. They only made my anger grow. Kayden knew how important seeing him every night had become to me, didn't he? I'd slept with my webcam on for over a month, always able to roll over and see him or talk to him. Not tonight. I felt unimportant.

Kayden and I had sent songs to express our feelings to each other throughout our relationship. I wanted to hurt him like he hurt me tonight. I selected a song that I knew would be a punch to his gut. I sent him the link to "Never There" by Cake. It was a brutal song, but it conveyed my feelings perfectly at the moment. Let him choke on it for a bit. I hit send.

"Fuck it. I'm going to bed, Suzy." I couldn't tell Suzy what I just sent to Kayden. I already regretted it.

"Okay, but he'll call. It'll all work out," she said with sadness in her eyes.

"I'll see you in the morning. Thanks, Suzy." I walked toward my room, staring at my phone, wishing I could cancel my last message.

I crawled into bed, cocooning myself in the blankets, and shut the world out. My eyes grew heavy from the never-ending tears.

I tossed and turned all night, unable to stop my mind from thinking the worst. I checked my phone over a dozen times, but Kayden never replied. I must have drifted off at some point because the next thing I knew, the clock read ten in the morning

I forced myself to get up. I needed caffeine. I felt numb, and my mind was hazy. I heard my phone chirp from where I stood in the kitchen. I turned my attention away from the brewing pot to the hallway. I wanted to run to see if it was Kayden, but I didn't want to seem too eager. He'd turned me into a crazy person in a short time. I'd never acted like this before with anyone. I walked slowly to my room and grabbed my phone, unable to resist the urge to talk to him any longer.

Kayden: Morning, beautiful. Sorry I fell asleep last night.

How should I respond to him? I didn't know what to say or how to deal with someone like him.

Kayden: WTF with the song, babe?

I swallowed hard because I knew it was a scathing song. I knew it would hurt him. When I sent it, I didn't give a fuck.

Me: It fit how I felt last night. I'm sorry.

Kayden: It's mean. It starts out sweet, but it was like a slap in the face.

I felt like a total piece of shit. He had a shitty day, and I was being a bitch.

Me: You didn't just fall asleep last night, Kayden.

Kayden: I know. We were talking and drinking, and I came in my room to call you, but I must have passed out or fallen asleep.

Me: Why didn't you call this morning instead of text? Have a hangover?

I knew my remark sounded snide, but I couldn't stop myself. I wanted to be the one he turned to and the one he leaned on.

Kayden: A bit. Let me get up and get myself straight, and I'll call you in a bit.

Me: Fine, but don't forget about me this time.

Kayden: I could NEVER forget about you.

I already felt left behind, forgotten.

Me: Felt like it last night.

Kayden: I'm sorry, Sophia. I'll make it up to you.

Me: Call me in a bit. I'm going to have some coffee, and I have things to do.

Kayden: Okay, baby doll. I'll talk to you in a bit.

I wanted to throw my phone or slap him in the face. The anger inside me hadn't subsided from last night.

Me: Okay. I'll be around.

Kayden: I love you.

I knew he loved me, but I didn't feel important anymore. He always made me feel like I was the center of his universe, a vital part of his day, but that feeling had vanished.

Me: Love you too.

I dressed, grabbed my coffee, and headed for the door. I wanted to keep myself busy today. It was a Saturday, and I hoped Kayden and I would spend much of the day Skyping. He never had a day off when we were apart, and I wanted to take advantage of every minute available. I wanted to get my errands done quickly to free up my afternoon for him.

My phone rang a couple hours later on the way to my last stop. Kayden's name appeared on my screen, and my heart thumped in my chest like it always did when seeing his name. He hadn't forgotten about me.

"Hey," he said.

"Hi. Whatcha been doing?" I asked.

"Listening to this fucking song," he slurred.

Fuck! Was he drunk? My heart sank.

"Have you been drinking already?"

"A bit, but I can't stop listening to this song. It's so fucking mean, Sophia."

174

"Jesus, really? How much have you had already?"

"Enough." I heard "Never There" in the background.

"Fucking amazing. I can't believe you are drinking this early, Kayden." I closed my eyes, a sense of doom filling me. "Call me back when you get sober." I clicked off the phone.

It was early, and he had already drunk enough for it to affect him. Was this how he handled a crisis? What more didn't I know about Kayden—drinking alone and drinking heavily? He disappeared again. I assumed he passed out. I finished my errands and returned home.

Throughout the day, sporadic text messages popped up on my phone from Kayden, none of them making sense. He never stuck around long enough to hold a conversation; although I doubt he had the ability to form a coherent thought.

"Hey." Suzy knocked on my bedroom door.

"Come in, Suzy."

"Let's go. Get ready. The girls will be here in an hour. We're all going out," Suzy stated firmly.

"I don't feel like it, Suzy." I shook my head.

"You're not sitting here all night waiting for him. Up, come on." She pulled my arm to get me moving.

I thought about it for a moment. I didn't want to sit home and worry about him. He didn't seem to worry about me. Suzy was right. I needed to get out and enjoy some time with my girls.

CHELLE BLISS

"Okay. I'll get ready," I said, climbing off my bed to rifle through my closet.

Kayden had a bottle of booze to keep him company. I had my girlfriends to fill the void caused by his total absence. I'd be damned if I'd stay home sitting by the phone and waiting for his call.

* * *

Worried about Kayden, I booked a flight to New Orleans on Friday. I needed to be with him, and he needed to be with me.

I'd always told myself I would never get involved with anyone who was an addict. I'd always steered clear of drugs in my life, but alcohol was everywhere. Could he control himself, or was he an alcoholic?

I wanted to think that if he was, I had the ability to save him. I wanted to be the good in his life that made him want to change. I needed to talk with him and find out exactly what was happening. I loved Kayden, and I was in too deep to turn my back on him.

When the plane touched down, I found a cab driver willing to take me to his apartment. I was so nervous and hadn't talked to Kayden since yesterday. I stared out the window and rubbed my sweaty palms together. *Was I crazy to show up unannounced?* I had to know he was okay. I had to see it for myself. I texted Kayden a few times during the drive but received no response. The taxi pulled into the parking lot where it all began—our first kiss and all the happiness and joy that I felt we would have together.

I walked to the door, hoping someone would be home to let me in. I knocked on the door and heard voices in murmured tones and laughing. I waited a moment before knocking again.

"Oh...hey, Sophia. What are you doing here?" Tom said as he began to close the door a little bit, so I couldn't see the entire living room.

"I need to see Kayden." I started to push against the door.

"He's not here," he said as he began to push back.

"I know he is, jerk. Just move out of my way," I said as I pushed the door open. His truck's in the parking lot. I just had to get to him.

Tom moved away after I pushed him into the wall behind the door. I walked through the apartment with all the men looking at me strangely. They all said hey to me but were on edge. I felt their eyes on my back as I reached Kayden's door, but none of them tried to stop me. I thought about knocking, but I wanted to surprise him. I slowly turned the handle to make it as quiet as possible. I walked through the doorway and stopped dead in my tracks.

What the fuck?

Kayden was lying in bed, but he wasn't alone. There was a girl snuggled up to him, and neither of them woke when I walked in.

I stood there for a moment and just stared. I recognized her from his postings on Facebook, but he said they were only friends. She must have been one of his girls before I became his *only* girl.

Her body was smashed against his with her arm draped over his stomach. She was wearing a tiny black tank top, but their lower bodies were covered by blankets except for their bare feet, tangled together.

I didn't make a sound...stunned and heartbroken. The sight in front of me squeezed my heart, crushing it. I had worried about him, flying to be by his side, but he had found solace in the arms of another. I walked backward and closed the door to rid my eyes of the vision of Kayden and *her*.

Tom tried to stop me and explain, but what could he say? I didn't want to hear it. I walked out, not looking back. Tears began to fall as I let myself feel the pain of his betrayal.

Keep walking, just keep walking. My mind was a jumble of emotions and numbness. I walked to the main street and hailed a cab.

"Where to?" the cab driver asked.

I fought through the tears to steady my voice, "Bourbon Street, please."

"You okay, lady?"

"I will be," I responded. I didn't know where else to go. I needed a drink and wanted to forget the horrible image that was burned in my eyes.

I had enough time on the drive to try to regain my composure, fix my makeup, and gather my thoughts.

"Can you drop me at the Funky Pirate, please?" I requested.

The streets were filled with people stumbling and celebrating; the nightly party thrived. I needed the excitement and liquor to make me forget. I climbed out of the cab and grabbed my small overnight bag. I hadn't brought much with me, thinking Kayden and I would spend the weekend in bed.

I was a fool. I found an empty seat at the bar, and the space was filled with happiness. A blues band played, and people were singing along, enjoying the funky music filling the air.

"A shot of vodka, please, and a chocolate martini," I said to the female bartender. She placed the martini in front of me moments later. I stared at it for a moment before taking a large gulp. I swallowed it, slamming the glass back on the counter.

"Another martini, please," I said to the bartender before she could walk away. Tears began to stream down my face. She placed the small glass filled with the vodka in front of me, but before her hands were totally free of the glass, I grabbed it. I downed it, feeling the warmth ooze throughout my body.

I felt the presence of someone standing beside me. I set the glass on the bar top before turning my head. A handsome man dressed in business attire watched me intently, studying my face.

"Can I help you?" I asked in a snotty voice.

"May I?" he asked, pointing to the stool next to me.

I rolled my eyes. "It's free, isn't it?"

"A pretty lady shouldn't be drinking alone in this town," he said, sitting down and calling over the waitress.

"Another for each of us," he said.

"I'll take another shot please," I told her. I needed the alcohol and a lot of it. I didn't care about anything but forgetting the entire night.

"What's wrong? Maybe I can help," he inquired.

"You can't help," I replied while staring at the bartender, hoping her feet would move faster.

He touched my hand, but I didn't move away from his touch. "Maybe I can."

"It will take a lot more liquor to accomplish that task," I said as I wiped a tear away from my cheek.

"What happened?"

"You don't want to hear my sad story."

"Yes, I do. Tell me, maybe I can help you," he said.

I stared into his eyes, studying him.

"I flew here to surprise my boyfriend, but when I got to his place, he was in bed with another woman." I downed the drink and set the glass down in front of me.

"That's horrible. How could he cheat on an amazing creature such as you?" he asked.

I rolled my eyes. He'd done this before. I didn't give a shit at that moment. I needed to share my story, let out my anger. "I guess I wasn't enough for him. I should have known he was a whore and wouldn't change his ways. I'm a fucking fool." The tears began to stream down my face once again. I grabbed the martini and gulped it. The liquor warmed my body. My legs grew numb, and my mind became a jumbled mess.

He reached for my cheek and wiped away a tear with his thumb. "He's the fool. I would love for a woman to fly to see me, someone who loved me enough to travel a great distance for my company."

I leaned into his palm—needing the physical connection. I closed my eyes, and images of Kayden flooded the darkness. We'd spent time in this bar—kissing, touching, laughing, and drinking.

"Another drink?" he asked.

My eyes flew open, and the happy memories evaporated. I reached into my purse and looked at my phone. I'd missed a dozen phone calls and more texts from Kayden. I turned it off, putting it back in my purse.

The handsome gentleman kept the drinks flowing, and numbness was soon filling my entire body and soul. Everything around me moved in slow motion. Staring in the mirror behind the bar, I tried bringing my face into focus, but I couldn't make out any of my features.

A hand covered mine to bring my attention back to my surroundings.

I turned to the gentleman and pleaded, "Kiss me, make me forget."

He turned my chair toward his, placing his hand on my neck. He paused for a moment, staring into my eyes—I didn't speak.

His lips touched mine, hard and wet. I thought it would help me forget, but my mind played a private movie of Kayden and his kiss. I craved him. He intoxicated me. This kiss made me feel nothing but an emptiness that couldn't be filled. *This was wrong*.

"What the fuck are you doing?" a man screamed.

The body of the stranger lurched away from mine, and my eyes flew open. I tried to focus, but just keeping them open was a struggle. The handsome gentleman was falling to the floor, and someone was moving on top of him. He looked like Kayden, but I had to be seeing things.

The businessman was being pummeled, and I couldn't do anything but watch. My head felt heavy as I placed it on the bar and tried to stop the room from spinning until darkness consumed me.

kayden

SOMEONE WAS SHAKING ME. "Dude, get the fuck up."

My stomach turned with the motion and the liquor sloshing around in my stomach. "Leave me the fuck alone. Go away."

"Fucker, Sophia was just here. She ran out."

Sophia. My heart pounded in my chest, increasing the feeling of nausea that overcame my body. Someone's body was wrapped around mine, and it wasn't Sophia.

"What the fuck?" I sat up quickly, throwing her legs off of mine.

"What the fuck are you doing here and in my bed?" I asked her.

"Tom called me. He thought you needed to talk to someone. You were passed out when I got here, and I thought I would sleep until you woke up," she said.

I felt like my world was ending. Everything unraveled while I lay here passed out. "Are you fucking crazy? That's not okay. You can't just crawl in my bed... ever. Fuck." I shook my head painfully.

"Where's Sophia?" I asked, panic lacing my voice.

I called her phone, but there was no answer. She wouldn't pick up the phone. I learned that once about Sophia. I needed to find her. New Orleans was the type of city that could swallow a girl like her.

"I don't know. I saw her jump in a cab," Tom said.

"Which cab? Maybe I can find out where they took her."

* * *

I couldn't believe my eyes. A man had his lips on Sophia, my Sophia. My body moved on its own, and I was unable to stop myself. I grabbed the man and threw him to the floor. My fist connected with his face, crunching the bones. Blood splattered on my hand and arms as I wailed on him, unable to stop.

I didn't look at Sophia as I beat this asshole to a pulp. I needed to destroy him as he had destroyed me, taking what was mine. Hands wrapped around me, pulling me off of him, but my arms continued to swing.

The man wiped the blood away from his face as he began to stand. "Dude, what the fuck?"

"What the fuck, asshole? You're kissing my girlfriend with your hands all over her, and you're asking me what the fuck," I said, ready to beat him again.

"She asked me to," he said with a smirk on his face, wiping the last bit of blood with the back of his hand.

"Just leave, take the girl, and get out of here," the bar employee said.

I walked over to Sophia, her head resting on the bar. I scooped her into my arms as her head fell back, mouth falling open. She looked a wreck, and I'd been the sole cause. I carried her to the car and brought her home to my bed.

I couldn't crawl into bed with her. Anger filled me, anger with myself and directed at her too. The good-girl quality of Sophia had drawn me to her. What she did tonight didn't fit with her nature. I sat in a chair in the corner of the room and watched her as she slept. I prayed she would understand and forgive me. I had driven her into the stranger's arms. I sat there all night, watching, waiting.

Morning light streamed through the window as I rested my elbows on my legs and placed my head in my palms. I sensed movement from the bed.

Looking up, I saw Sophia blinking, trying to clear her eyes. She stared at me but didn't say a word. I couldn't hold my tongue any longer. I needed to know and needed to move on. I needed us.

"What the fuck were you thinking?" I asked, my voice seething in anger.

"I could ask you the same thing," she spat back.

"I find you in a bar, drunk, kissing a stranger, and his hands are all over you! You weren't struggling to get away but seemed to be enjoying yourself."

"Am I supposed to feel sorry for you, Kayden? I fucking don't. I walked in yesterday to find you not alone. So don't give me some bullshit about kissing a stranger," she said, sitting up straighter.

"Nothing happened with her and me. I was already passed out when she got here, and she crawled in my bed on her own. I never even woke up until after you left, and the guys woke me up. They called her to come over, not me, thinking I needed someone to talk to. She's a friend and only a friend. I did nothing wrong, Sophia. I didn't touch her, let alone place my lips on hers," I said, sadness filling me with the image of Sophia kissing another man.

"I don't believe you! I saw your tangled bodies, naked in this very bed."

"I told you already. I was passed out and never even knew she was here. Does she want me? Yes. Do I want her? Fuck no," I yelled. "Nothing happened between us, but I clearly saw your lips on another man. You ripped my heart out. I never thought you would do that, Sophia."

A knock sounded at the door, but we kept our eyes locked on each other.

"What?"

"Can I come in?" Tom asked.

"What the fuck?" she said, throwing her hands in the air.

The door opened slowly, and he entered the room, looking around and gulping loudly.

"Sophia, I need to explain," Tom spoke to her, approaching the bed.

"Save it, Tom. I know what I saw," she said to him, keeping her eyes pointed at me.

"I know what you think you saw, but it's not what happened. Kayden never woke up. He has been passed out most of the week. The only time he was up was to find his next drink. I called her to talk to him. We all work together, and they've been friends for years. I thought she could get through to him. I didn't know that she would end up falling asleep in his bed," Tom stated.

"You really think I'm going to believe that?"

"It's the truth. I was trying to get him on track, for you, Sophia. I never thought she'd take advantage of the situation. When I arrived home from work, Kayden was already passed out cold. She showed up and went into his room. He didn't do anything with her. He loves you and wouldn't cheat on you," he pleaded with Sophia.

"Thanks for telling me, Tom. Kayden and I need to discuss last night if you don't mind," she said.

"I am being honest with you. He needs you, Sophia," Tom said as he stood up and moved toward the door.

I'd remained silent while Tom spoke. My eyes never left hers, conveying hurt and anguish. She dropped her head into her hands and began to cry. *I had fucked everything up.*

I said nothing and didn't move to comfort her. We both did wrong, but I needed her to speak to me first.

"I was mad at you for drinking so much and pushing me away. I hate myself for running away and into the arms of another man, but you need to know what last night did to me." She looked up at me, into me, through me. "You'd been absent and drinking. I thought you had been drinking and fucking your way through your days and nights. I'm such a whore for kissing that man in the bar."

"Sophia, I can't believe you'd think that of me. I'd never. I'm sorry I allowed the alcohol to consume me, become my lifeline."

"I'm sorry, Kayden. I don't know what else to say," she cried into her palms.

"Sophia," I said, moving toward her. I sat on the bed and pulled her hands away from her face. "You thought I fucked the girl in my bed, and you were upset. I've been acting like a total asshole."

"You had me out of my mind. I was so worried about you, and then I found you in bed with someone else. It was an image I just couldn't get out of my brain."

I wiped the tears away from her face. "I will always be faithful to you. I'm yours, and you're mine. No matter what you think you saw, I'm not a cheater. I'm a one-woman man. I will not share you either."

"I wasn't thinking clearly last night after having so many drinks. I'm sorry."

"I know what that's like, trust me," I said with a smile. "We've hurt each other, Sophia. I hurt you with my drinking and not being there, and you hurt me by allowing someone else to kiss you. If it weren't for my behavior, you wouldn't have allowed another man to touch you."

"Never. I should have stayed and fought with you, for you."

"You should have hit me or yelled...anything other than running away and into the arms of another man."

"I'll never do that again. I have never loved another soul deeper and harder than I love you," she said to me.

"I love you, too, Sophia," I said, kissing her lips. I undressed and crawled under the covers with her. I needed to feel her skin against mine.

I'd never been so utterly in love with a person. I wanted her, and more importantly, I needed her. I felt that the bottle was my only friend, holding my hand, helping me through this journey. It was easy to fall back on bad habits that had been there to console me in the past. Alone in this apartment, booze became my only friend and solace. I shut Sophia out and nearly paid the ultimate price.

I could almost touch the strain between us. Our actions had caused a crack that needed to be mended.

I kissed her with all the emotion and love I felt in my heart. I needed to be inside her, remind her of my love. I made love to Sophia, face-to-face. I looked into her big brown eyes and never looked away. I needed the connection with her. She was mine, and I was hers.

We spent most of Saturday inside holding each other and made love once.

"Please, promise me you won't drink like that again, Kayden," she asked in a pleading voice.

"I'm sorry," I responded. I didn't know if I could hold true to a promise like that, and all I could do was apologize.

"You scared me. I've missed you the past week. I don't think I could do that again," she said sternly.

"I used to have a drinking problem and sought help after my arrest, but I have it under control."

"I had no idea," she said sadly.

"That's because I never mentioned it. I don't usually say, 'Hey, I'm Kayden, and I'm an alcoholic.' I had it under control. I don't usually drink so much... I'm just so depressed about not working. My life is falling apart," I replied with sorrow in my voice. Sophia was my one bright spot, but I couldn't focus on her, and the darkness was outweighing the light.

"Please try not to drink...for me. Be constructive. You've spent days drunk and passed out. You should have been using that time to fight. Promise me, Kayden. Your life isn't falling apart. I'm still here. Don't forget about me," she said harshly.

sophia

I WOULDN'T SAY he currently had anything under control. Control was a word addicts used when they still abused their drug of choice. The addiction usually controlled the person, not the other way around. I would say, this last week, his addiction, namely vodka, had controlled him.

"I'm sorry, and I promise to do better. I never want to upset you," he said, staring into my eyes before kissing me on the cheek.

I understood that he felt sad and that he loved his job, but instead of drinking himself into oblivion, he should've been making phone calls and figuring out his next step. If there was no hope, as he assumed, then he needed to decide what to do next. *Please let it involve me.*

Exhaustion painted his face. The weight of the

world was on his shoulders, but I wanted him to know he wasn't alone. I would be there for him and help him in any way I could. The weekend passed quickly, and I needed to go home to return to work.

I had been so scared and helpless while I was away from him. If he was drunk and passed out, he would not be able to make decisions about his future or look for alternate employment. I wanted him in my life, but I did not sign up for a relationship with vodka. I would not give up on him. He needed to understand the depths of my sadness and worry.

He squeezed me tightly, and I got out of bed to pack my suitcase. My heart told me everything would be all right, but my mind knew better. I knew this wasn't the end of his struggle with alcohol. I knew a decision would have to be made. Did I stay and be his rock, or did I run and cause him to spiral even further?

At the airport, we kissed good-bye. Tears streamed down my face, and I could barely breathe. I felt like my world was ending as I hugged him, unable to let go. I inhaled him. He smelled like the man who I had always smelled before, instead of the stale vodka scent that lingered on his skin yesterday.

I cried walking through security.

I'd miss him. More importantly, I was scared— scared that the drinking would cause our relationship to fall apart.

This was the point where most people would walk

away. Where someone would say run, but I couldn't do that. I believed he could be fixed. That my love could change him, heal him, and make everything okay. I wouldn't give up on that possibility, and I wouldn't give up on Kayden now.

kayden

I HADN'T BEEN ENTIRELY truthful with Sophia in the beginning. I had a drinking problem. Up until about two years ago, my life had been filled with addiction to alcohol or drugs. The aftermath with Lisa caused me to gain control. It was not out of want, though. It was out of necessity. Sophia only knew a small snippet of my past.

My life had spiraled out of control for many years, but one positive thing that occurred because of my arrest was that I gained control of my drinking...until now.

I had nowhere else to turn after my arrest. I couldn't go home to my parents, and I had no means to support myself. I lost my job because I didn't show up the next day. I went to a homeless shelter run by the Salvation Army and lived in their communal housing where I was required to attend alcoholism counseling and work in their store. I had to take a real look at my life and what actions led to my ending up at their facility. The alcohol had caused so many problems throughout my life. It was my kryptonite. I had to stop it from ruling my life, and I had been successful until now.

I would eventually share all of the gory details with Sophia. I had to. I needed to. I had to wait for a time when I had control over my life. She was the only beacon of hope in my life. I would try to stay sober for her—try to be the better man she deserved.

I felt my world falling apart as she walked through security at the airport. I reassured her that everything would be okay, even though I didn't believe any of it.

What was I without a job?

Who was I?

I had lost my center and my reason for being, besides Sophia. I loved my work, and it helped keep my mind occupied when we weren't together.

What would I do without her here? The bottle would be my only friend nearby. I needed her with me, my moral compass. She deserved so much better than me, but I couldn't give her up. Ever.

I walked out of the airport and through the parking garage until I found my truck. Climbing inside, I closed the door, and I could still smell her perfume in the air. She was gone, and I was alone, again. I needed a fucking drink.

I was a complete and utter fucking mess.

sophia

KAYDEN SAID there were things I didn't know about him. I never thought alcoholism would be one. The signs were there. He always had a drink in his hand, and there was never a day totally alcohol-free when we were together. I always ended up drunk or buzzed, while he remained unfazed.

I loved Kayden, but I'd be lying if I didn't admit my emotions were mixed with the knowledge of his alcohol abuse. How could I walk away from him? I could not even go a night without talking to him. When he was clean and working, I adored the man. How did I not know this about him?

Could I deal with a man who had a drinking problem? Someone who went to the bottle and buried his head instead of fighting for what he wanted? I didn't want that life for myself. My mom had three traits she warned me against constantly: don't marry a drug addict, a cheater, or a drinker. While I didn't always want to listen to my mom, and often rebelled against her advice, in the end, she was usually right.

Kayden promised me he would try not to drink so much, but who was I fucking kidding? An addict can't just stop with a mere promise. His drinking started again, possibly before the wheels of my plane touched the tarmac. He had no chance of staying sober since drinking was the norm among the guys. I saw the bottles lined up on the counter: tequila, vodka, rum, and whiskey. They were the only form of decoration. The temptation too great for him to deny. I had a choice to make.

The Kayden I knew and loved had disappeared.

In his place, there was a man consumed with despair, often missing from my day. Time ticked away. I filled my days as I had before, immersing myself in books and my work. Each day, I prayed for normalcy. It had been established the day he entered my world, invaded it, more accurately, and now there was a hole where he used to be.

Me: Ready to Skype, sweetness?

Kayden: I think I'm dying.

I sighed. The everyday drama exhausted me.

Me: Huh?

Me: You okay?

No response. *Fucking asshole. I'm dying* aren't the last words you want to hear from someone before they disappear. My heart sank, and I felt physically ill. Our talks and seeing him online each evening used to be the best part of my day, and now everything had changed.

As much as my life had shifted the day I met him, it had spun on its axis again, and everything seemed to be unraveling. He wrecked me. Not a quick stab to the heart, but a slow dissection with a dull, rusty blade.

I drowned my sorrows in the lives of my favorite fictional characters and tried to lose myself in their blissful lives, but Kayden never strayed from my thoughts. Kayden would emerge when his self-induced coma wore off sometime tomorrow. Mental and physical exhaustion took over and allowed me to dream of the love I was missing.

* * *

My phone chirped, and I wanted to ignore him, but I couldn't. The pull was too strong.

Kayden: Are you mad at me?

He left me hanging, worried and stressed, and I wanted to punch him in the face and I wasn't a violent person.

Me: More than I can explain right now.

Kayden: I'm sorry.

I knew he meant those words, but my anger drove my words.

Me: You're always sorry, Kayden, but you aren't doing anything about it.

Kayden: What do you want me to do?

I clenched my jaw, wanting to scream, but I held it in.

Me: Come up with a plan, something besides getting lost in a bottle.

Kayden: If I don't get my job back, then I'm coming to you, Sophia.

Didn't he want to be with me? I didn't want to be a last resort. My heart fractured a little deeper. My love for this man had eclipsed anything I'd ever felt before for anyone.

Me: You're going to get it back. I just know it.

Kayden: It's highly unlikely. I'm fucking losing my mind here, Sophia... I can't do this anymore.

Me: What?

Kayden: I can't be without you anymore. I won't do it. I'm going to lean on you, Sophia. I need your light to pull me out of the darkness.

Me: I want you to lean on me, confide in me, but you've leaned on Jack for weeks. I'm afraid I'd be just another crutch. I remember something you said to me once—we all fall sometimes in life, Sophia. It's more important how we recover.

Kayden: I don't know how to recover. I'm used to leaning on the bottle. It's been my only friend at times.

My limit reached, I lashed out at him.

Me: I can't do this anymore, Kayden. You aren't thinking of what this is doing to me. When you get yourself straight, come back to me.

Kayden: You're breaking up with me?

Me: If it gets you clean, then yes.

Kayden: Fuck off, then.

There it was. I was harsh with my words, but I didn't know what else to say to him. I had tried to be the understanding and loving girlfriend. I tried to be supportive and help keep his spirits hopeful. None of it worked. Maybe he needed to get pissed off at me, scared a bit. He needed to fight for something, anything...for me.

Me: Really? You don't choose me? Guess that's that. I'll fuck off, Kayden. Thanks for showing me what love could be, should be...even if only for a moment. Hope you find peace and happiness someday, just make sure it's not with Lisa.

Kayden: WTF with Lisa?

I knew the Lisa comment would catch his attention. God, this man brought out the shitty side of me. The one that wanted to fight. That wanted him to fight. No longer was I the meek and mild librarian, I was ready to throw down and cut a bitch for what I thought was worth fighting for.

Me: Whoever you are with in the future. Make sure it's not her. She made you miserable for too long.

Kayden: I'm completely happy with you, Sophia. I'm just not happy with me.

I'd do anything for this man. I needed him to understand that, to feel it.

Me: It's no excuse. You're making sure to push me the fuck away, aren't you?

Kayden: You're really breaking up with me?

My words were hollow, but I hoped it caused his heart to stop for a moment. I couldn't imagine my life without Kayden, his passion and love. Didn't he just tell me to fuck off? Having a conversation with a drunk was so futile. They spoke without thinking and then had amnesia within a few minutes. Why did I even bother?

Me: You told me to fuck off.

Kayden: I did, and I'm sorry. Can we start the day over? I love you, Sophia. I'll do better, try harder.

Me: Call me when you wake up and can talk to me, Kayden. I need to hear your voice today.

I placed my phone next to my pillow, wishing for sleep to take me. My eyes flew open with a chirp that I couldn't ignore. Kayden had sent me a song, and my heart thumped as I hit play. "The Reason" by Hoobastank filled the air. I listened carefully to the words, and they wrapped around me, stealing my breath.

kayden

LANDSLIDE

I KEPT FUCKING EVERYTHING UP. How did I let my life become ruled by alcohol? The one person I cared about more than anything in the world —Sophia—I had placed on the back burner. I had become selfish and thought only about myself. She was my happiness, and I focused too much on what had gone wrong instead of all the wonderful things that had fallen into my lap unexpectedly. I finally had something to look forward to for the first time in weeks—Sophia had booked a flight.

She would be here tomorrow, and the place was a mess. I was a mess. I needed to clean the apartment and stay sober—I could do it for her. I wouldn't choose the bottle over her. My phone chimed, and I ran to look at the message.

Sophia: What are you doing, baby?

Me: Starting to clean. This place is a pigsty, and the guys haven't bothered cleaning up after themselves.

Sophia: Not going to lie in bed and wallow in a bottle today?

Ouch. Fuck. I deserved that. She had no reason to believe in me anymore. I would have to earn her trust again.

Me: No, Soph. I'm staying sober. Done drinking. It hasn't solved any of my problems, just seemed to cause more. I need to start coming up with a plan for my future—our future.

Sophia: That's a good attitude. Hopefully, they aren't empty words.

I meant every word. I needed a plan, but somehow the bottle always called me, filled with false promises.

Me: I know you don't believe me, but I'll prove it to you. Just don't give up on me. Don't leave me.

I spent all day scrubbing floors, vacuuming, and cleaning the bathrooms. I went to the grocery store and purchased all her favorites. I dumped out the bottles of liquor I had in my bedroom and moved Tom's bottles into his room. I couldn't stare at his bottles and have the temptation in plain view.

Sophia: I've missed you.

Me: I've been here all along.

Sophia: You haven't been the man I fell in love with. You've been noticeably absent in my life.

Me: I'm back, Sophia. I can't even explain how happy I

am that you'll be here tomorrow. You're the most important thing in my life.

She was everything to me. She made me feel whole. I had been acting like a fucking fool and a selfish prick. I'd be devastated without her. A job was just that—a job. I could find another job or line of work. As long as I had Sophia by my side, I could do anything. I wanted to be worthy of her love.

I didn't think Sophia had any experience with an alcoholic. She couldn't understand what my body was battling.

I'd been going through withdrawals all day, and I prayed they stopped before she arrived. I looked like shit and felt even worse. My body shook uncontrollably. I knew a drink would take the edge off, but I couldn't take the chance of falling down the rabbit hole.

I needed to deal with the effects of withdrawal naturally and not with a Bloody Mary.

sophia

GOOD-BYE NOLA

I NEEDED TO TOUCH HIM—REMIND
him of what he had to fight for. We were made for
each other and brought together at this moment in
time for a reason. I needed his passion, and Kayden
needed a constant. Our experiences molded us into
people who fit perfectly together. He couldn't throw
that away, and I sure as hell wasn't going to allow him
to do it either.

My heart raced, almost bursting out of my chest,
as I walked through the airport. Walking out past
security, I could see Kayden waiting for me. Leaning
against a wall, he looked nervous and a little worn
down. He smiled sweetly when he saw me and looked
handsome as always in jeans, a T-shirt, and sandals.
My pace quickened. I couldn't wait another second to
be wrapped in his arms. I inhaled him and was
bombarded with a mix of smells—stale vodka and the

man I loved.

I looked up into his beautiful, sad green eyes. "You haven't been drinking today, have you?" I couldn't help but ask, scared to get in his truck if he had. I held my breath, waiting for him to answer.

"Not today, baby doll," he replied. As he squeezed me tighter, I could feel his body shaking.

"You're shaking, Kayden. Are you all right?"

"I'm great. I'm just so excited and happy to see you," he said smoothly.

Bullshit. He'd never shaken before. He was no more excited this time than he had been before. I knew the symptoms of withdrawals, his body craving alcohol. He needed it. My heart sank with the knowledge that he had been experiencing physical pain. Was he a full-blown alcoholic—always been an alcoholic—or had the last couple weeks just taken a toll on his body?

We'd never stayed home during our time together. We always found our way to a bar or a club. I guess the signs had been there, but I never made the connection.

He grabbed my bag and held my hand as we walked to his truck. Quiet filled the air during our walk. Would we start this trip the same as we always had before? Our relationship wasn't merely physical, but we needed it like the air we breathed. He threw my bag in his truck. He turned around, faced me, and drew me into a soul-sucking kiss. I'd missed his commanding kisses, searing touch, and suffocating

passion. I needed the reassurance that we were okay—
that he was okay.

He turned my body away from his and pushed me
against the hood of his truck. I could hear the zipper of his
pants moving quickly. Was he really going to fuck me
right here in the open? My heart pounded with the fear of
being caught. It sounded like thunder filling my ears.
Cool air caressed my flesh as he lifted the back of my
dress. Placing his hand on my shoulder, he used the
leverage to push his hard cock inside me. I rested my
hands on the hood, trying to find anything to hold on to.
This is the man I knew, the one who was so filled with lust
and longing that he couldn't wait to be buried inside me.

I couldn't focus on our surroundings. Were there
other people nearby? Cameras? My mind raced with
thoughts, but the battering of his cock drove all
rational thinking from my brain. I was mindless with
lust and longing for Kayden. I only cared about the
feeling of him inside me and his skin grazing my ass.
He held both of my shoulders, rendering me immobile,
unrelenting in his pursuit of release.

His breathing quickened and turned erratic as his
body shook. "Fuck," he moaned. He filled me with his
warmth as his body became limp against my back.

"Jesus." I had never been so reckless in my life, and
I couldn't think of another word to express my
surprise. He pulled his cock out of me, causing his
come to run down my inner thigh. I lay there in shock

for a moment before moving. Had I just allowed him to fuck me outside? I loved when Kayden went all caveman, when he took me without asking, ravaged my body, and used me entirely.

Kayden turned my limp body, propping my back against the truck, and kissed me deeply. His kiss conveyed all the emotions he felt in that moment—love, lust, sadness, longing, and comfort. Breaking the kiss, he stared into my eyes. "I love you, Sophia. I'm in love with you, consumed, head over heels. My life would end without you... I need you. Don't ever leave me, Sophia."

Lost in his eyes and absorbed in the emotion of the moment, I caressed his face. "I'm yours...always," I said. "I've searched my entire life for you, and I'm not willing to throw you away so easily. Don't shut me out anymore."

He rested his forehead against mine with his eyes closed. "I never shut you out. I don't know how to explain it to you. The darkness that consumes me is caused by you not being here. My work helped keep my mind and body occupied in your absence, but without you to touch and hold...I have nothing. The bottle became my only comfort. It has been a constant in my life." He paused and swallowed hard before continuing, "I've always been discarded or used by women, but I've used them for my own pleasure as well. After being hurt so much, I knew I could only rely on myself. My heart hardened, and I became a user. You changed my world, Sophia."

"I love you, Kayden," I said, kissing his lips tenderly. "Take me home."

* * *

We spent the weekend enjoying the French Quarter and New Orleans without drinking. I didn't ask to go to Bourbon Street or anything revolving around liquor. The temptation would be too great for Kayden, and it would be unfair of me to put him in that position. The city had so much more to offer: culture, art, quaint coffee shops, unique stores, and historic sites—plenty to fill a lifetime without staggering into a bar.

I could understand why people lived here. It was old and romantic. The city parks and old churches added life and charm to this old town. The smells and sounds were intoxicating. The city had a history and a story to tell if you bothered to listen. The people were charming and kind, filled with Southern hospitality. We sat on the old church steps, enjoying some coffee, and watched the people move about their day. Kayden and I always talked so freely and openly, but all weekend, an invisible barrier separated us. I needed to hear his story, his secrets. I needed to know before I left. My heart sank at the thought of leaving this man behind. Could I leave him again?

"Kayden, you keep saying you have things to tell

me about your past... Can you share them with me? It's not fair to keep dangling them in front of me and never share the details," I pleaded.

"I've just tried to shelter you from my past. I don't think you can ever imagine what my life has been like. It's so much worse than you can imagine," he said.

I grabbed his hand, enclosing it in mine. "Kayden, I love you for everything you are now, not for what you were. I want to know all of you, what made you into the man you are today, the man who has consumed my every thought and captured my soul."

He lifted my fingers to his lips, kissing them. "I struggled with drugs in my youth, every kind imaginable. My life consisted of getting my next fix, booze, and women." Opening my palm, he nuzzled his face into the warmth of my hand. "My marriage ended because of my drinking. My wife, Danielle, made me so absolutely miserable that drinking was the only thing I looked forward to in my day. I met Lisa shortly after my marriage ended, and she wrapped me up in her world. I already told you how that ended. Fuck, she was a manipulative bitch. After my arrest, I had nowhere to go. Lisa had driven every person I loved out of my life. My mom didn't want anything to do with me. I was truly alone. I lived in a homeless shelter, and they enrolled me in their alcohol abuse program. I worked in their store in exchange for a roof over my head. It was the single lowest point in my life," he said.

"I tried hard the last year to be a better man and stay on the straight and narrow. I need to feel a purpose in life, keep myself occupied. My job was my purpose for so long, and then you came into my life. My life was simple before you: work, sleep, eat, and repeat. Sometimes, I'd call someone for a night of lust but no further attachments. You sucked me in and consumed my every thought. Every time I have to say good-bye to you, a small piece of my heart breaks. Without work to keep me busy and with you so far away...I feel lost," he told me.

I couldn't leave Kayden behind. I wouldn't do it. I turned to him and said, "You're coming home with me tonight, Kayden."

"I don't have the money to pay for a ticket." He shook his head. "I can't go. I used my savings to pay the balance of my restitution to Lisa, so my name is finally cleared and so is my record."

"You have a credit for the ticket you had to cancel last month because of the hurricane. We can use that, and I'll cover the difference. I'm not leaving you here alone," I said, looking him in the eye.

He thought about it before responding. "I don't know. I don't want to be a burden on you, Sophia. Without a job, I don't have any money to buy food or pay for anything," he said to me with a sincere look on his face.

"I can't leave you here without any way to eat or

survive," I said as I brushed my fingertips against his cheek.

"The guys will make sure I'm fed," Kayden said.

"They'll also make sure you're drunk, too. I *want* to be with you. We can spend more than a weekend together for once. I can fall asleep in your arms each night. We've always been so rushed. When you're rehired, I'll get you back to New Orleans," I promised, pleading with him.

"I hate having to rely on anyone, Sophia."

"Stop the macho bullshit. We never have enough time together."

"Okay, I'll come with you."

I knew he loved this city and his life was here, but I was his life, too. I was the only one who could help him, motivate him, and keep him on track. I was not and never had been a drinker. He needed to get away from the guys, the nightly drinking, and break the pattern.

That evening he packed a bag and told his roommate he would be gone until he could return to work. I felt at peace knowing he would be with me. No more wondering what happened to him, if he was okay, or if he was drinking.

Sadness showed on his face as we drove through the city, heading toward the airport. "You'll be back, Kayden—this is only temporary."

"I love this city, but I want to be with you. I wish we lived here together," he said.

I squeezed his hand, knowing we would be back. Our time in New Orleans wasn't over just yet. We made the flight bound for Florida. Kayden was fidgeting in his seat on the plane. "What's wrong, baby?" I asked.

"I hate to fly."

"Really? You flew to see me and never mentioned it."

"I didn't want you to think I'm a pussy, but I loathe flying," he told me, looking out the window.

"I'll hold your hand. I hate flying, too. I was so scared once that they gave me a little pair of wings before I got off the plane."

"That's funny," he laughed.

I slapped his chest. "Quiet, mister." I rested my head against his shoulder, gripping his hand as the plane ascended. The cabin of the plane was dark, and the city lights twinkled outside the window.

"Wanna join the mile-high club?" he whispered in my ear.

I swallowed hard, thinking through his proposition before answering, "We can't. We'll get in trouble."

He chuckled at my words, "You're always worried about getting in trouble. Come on, the fear always makes it hotter."

"No, no. I can't! It's too scary," I said, shaking my head against his soft T-shirt.

The plane shook from turbulence, and Kayden flinched and grabbed the armrests. "Wow, you're more scared than me. Who knew I'd ever find someone more afraid of flying than I am?"

"Don't laugh. That shit's scary," he said.

I closed my eyes for the rest of the flight. Kayden stroked my arm, more for his comfort than mine. Exhaustion didn't even begin to explain what I felt, but I knew I would sleep in Kayden's arms tonight.

Kayden and I dropped our bags in my room and undressed. We crawled into bed, skin on skin, and I nestled against him.

"Good night, Kayden," I said, reaching up to kiss his lips, and then I nuzzled back into his chest.

"Night, Sophia. I love you," he replied as he kissed the top of my head. I reached up and scratched his goatee. I tangled my fingers in his facial hair until I felt his body twitch before slipping into my own oblivion.

kayden

MAKING A HOME

I COULD FEEL Sophia crawling out of bed to turn off the screeching alarm. She was trying to not wake me, but the alarm volume had done the job for her. I watched her dress by the glow of the television. I waited for a kiss, but she started to creep toward the door.

"Morning, beautiful, were you going to leave without giving me a kiss?" I asked her.

"Oh, baby. I wanted to let you sleep," she said, turning around.

"Don't ever leave without kissing me and saying good-bye."

"I'm sorry. I won't do it again."

"Kiss me."

"Always, love. I wish I didn't have to go to work, but I'll be home on my break," she said to me as I lay there still waiting for a kiss. "Okay, Okay. You want a kiss. I got it." She leaned down and touched her lips to mine.

"Thank you," I said to her. "Have a good day at work. I'll see you on your break."

"Go back to sleep, handsome. Text me when you're awake," she said as she stood, heading for the door.

I closed my eyes and thought about how lucky I was to have Sophia in my life. Where would I have been at that moment without her? I missed work and New Orleans, of course, but I needed Sophia more than anything. I played our time together in my mind until I drifted back to sleep.

I texted Sophia went I woke up, as she asked.

Sophia: You doing okay?

Me: Better than I have in a long time, Sophia. Thank you for bringing me home.

I felt relieved to be away from New Orleans and at home with Sophia. I smelled her pillow, waiting for her reply.

Sophia: No place I'd rather you be than keeping my bed warm. No point in you being alone in New Orleans when we can spend time together. We never seem to have enough of it.

Me: I should've come weeks ago.

Sophia: I'm glad you're happy. We'll get your work all straightened out, and then you can return to New Orleans. But for now, I'm going to enjoy every moment we have together.

Me: I'm sorry I've been such a dick.

I didn't know what else to say to her—how to express my sorrow for my behavior the last few weeks. The only thing I could do was stay sober. It was easier to do being with Sophia. She had no liquor in the house, maybe by design, and she lived in the middle of nowhere. I had no form of transportation when she worked, and there were no stores within walking distance.

Me: *Anyway... I think I'm going to wash our clothes from the weekend. Is that okay?*

Sophia: *Hell yes. Hang your clothes up in my closet when you're done. What's mine is yours, Kayden.*

Me: *Be back in a bit.*

Sophia: *I have to get back to the kids anyway.*

I washed clothes and cleaned her room while waiting for her. I checked out the pantry and fridge to see what I could make for dinner. At least I could help out around the house and help keep her fed. Thankfully, Sophia didn't have to work late, giving us hours together in the evening.

Dinner simmered on the stove when Sophia walked through the door a little after three. She walked into her room, dropped her bags, and crawled into bed with me.

"What have you been doing?" she asked.

"Washed all the clothes, cleaned your bathroom, straightened up the room a bit, got dinner started, and waited for you," I replied.

"Wow, thanks. I've been a little preoccupied lately.

218

That leaves more time for just us," she said, snuggling her face into my neck.

We spent the evening in bed, shutting the world out. Sophia fell asleep early, but I didn't have the heart to wake her. Her soft breaths and tiny snores made me chuckle. I'd never heard her snore before tonight. I brushed the hair away from her face and stared at her perfection. Holding her closer, I kissed her eyes and smelled her.

A knock sounded at the door, but Sophia didn't move.

"Come in," I said quietly.

The door opened slowly, and a ragged Suzy appeared. "I'm so sick. I just wanted to let you know that I'm not going to work tomorrow."

"Okay, Suzy. If you need anything, just text me. This little one is out for the evening," I said, looking down at Sophia.

"She sleeps like a rock. I'm going to bed, and I'll see you in the morning, God willing." Suzy closed the door.

I picked up my tablet and snapped pictures of Sophia asleep in my arms. I didn't want a posed picture but something pure and honest. She looked like a child wrapped in my arms. Her innocence drew me to her, the pull stronger now than ever before.

I slowly moved her off of me, but she didn't even stir. I'd never seen someone sleep so soundly. I turned off the lights and crawled back in bed. I found a peace

CHELLE BLISS

with Sophia in my arms unlike any other I've experienced.

Sophia left for work early the next morning, and I took care of Suzy. I brought her soup and ice water in bed, making sure she didn't get up for anything. I was so thankful that she allowed me to stay with them. I wanted to help them in every way possible. They had given me a roof over my head when I needed it most and had nowhere else to turn.

Suzy, Sophia, and I slowly fell into a pattern. I often cooked dinner, and the three of us ate together. Some evenings we played cards and watched movies. We became a threesome, not sexually, but in friendship.

Suzy gave us our privacy, but we included her as much as possible. Sometimes she'd lay on the bed with us and talk. Sophia and I were both older, and she used the opportunity to pick our brains about love and life. Why she chose us to ask, I'll never understand. Sophia and I had failed miserably before finding each other. We could only offer her advice on what not to do. She became like a little sister, filled with questions, looking to me for answers.

I spent the next month applying to every place imaginable—job application after fucking job application. What a pain in the ass. Every single one wanted to know about my criminal record, and I answered honestly, but I knew I was doomed as soon as I hit send. I wished I could grab this shitty black cloud following me around and piss on it.

The holidays were closing in fast, and all I wanted was a drink. Every day was a struggle for me. It called to me. Every fucking day, it called to me. I needed to work, and the idleness of my life had become mind-numbing.

So much in my life was up in the air. Would I be able to stay in Florida with Sophia? I couldn't return to New Orleans without a job in place. I tried to live in the present and not worry about the future as Sophia had asked.

She told me, "Everything has a way of working out in the end." I loved her for her optimism, but I knew the realities.

sophia

TOM CALLED to tell Kayden the company would be closing down the apartment by the end of the month and that if he wanted his things, we needed to go there soon.

We left for New Orleans immediately. Sadness filled us as we drove to New Orleans. It would be a good-bye trip. Dread filled me the closer we got. I'd fallen in love with this city. It had become part of us.

I parked the car in the parking lot, and we sat for a moment. This was where we began. The love, passion, and crazy journey we'd experienced together.

Kayden looked around the parking lot, surveying the cars. "I don't see my truck, Sophia. It's missing," he said. I covered my eyes with my hands, and my stomach felt uneasy. "It must have been towed. I'll call them when we get inside."

"I'm sorry, baby," I said through my palms, feeling awful for him.

Kayden peeled my hands off my face. "Shit happens. I'll get it back. Come on," he said as he reached for the handle, and I did the same.

I held his hand as we approached the apartment. He paused before placing the key in the door. The apartment looked exactly like it did when we left in October, minus some personal effects and the television in the living room. A fold-up chair was propped against the wall, and some trash was strewn across the kitchen table.

I walked away from Kayden, turning the corner to his room. I stopped in the hallway. His bedroom door was open, and the door frame had been damaged. Someone had pried the door open. My heart sank as I walked through the door. "Your TV is missing!"

"What?" he asked as he rounded the corner behind me. Kayden came to a halt, staring blankly and not saying a word. The flat screen television no longer sat on his dresser beside his Blu-ray player. That was missing too, along with all of his movies. I heard rustling behind me as Kayden disappeared into his walk-in closet. "Motherfucker," he said.

I could hear things crashing to the floor. "What's wrong, baby?"

"All my fucking tools are gone. Everything is gone."

I wrapped my arms around him. "It can't all be gone."

223

CHELLE BLISS

"I'm okay. I told you I have a fucking black cloud following my ass around."

I grabbed his face, looking into his eyes, and kissed him. Not a lust-filled kiss but one filled with love and understanding. "We'll figure it out. We need to call the police," I said.

We searched his bedroom, taking inventory of everything that remained. It only took us a couple minutes to figure out that everything of value had vanished.

I felt responsible. I made him return to Florida with me. If he'd stayed in New Orleans, he'd still have his things. Though, we might not have survived as a couple if he did. I didn't think I could be any sadder than I was when we were driving here, but I never could have imagined this—Merry Christmas and Happy fucking New Year.

Kayden placed a call to the police to report a burglary. The kitchen had been stripped. The bathroom was cleared of everything except one towel and a partially used body wash, and his bedroom was ransacked. Even his jar of change had disappeared.

The police officers wrote down all the missing items and asked basic questions. They would file a report but didn't bother to take fingerprints from the doors or surfaces in the room. They gave us a copy of the report number in case Kayden needed it later. They said that his property had probably been sold off by now, and there was not much hope of recovering it.

224

He had nothing left but me.

"What do you want to do, Sophia?" he asked.

"I'm exhausted. Can we go to sleep and figure everything out tomorrow?" I asked him while rubbing my eyes.

"Yes, let me lock up tight first," he said as he checked the front door and then proceeded to the kitchen.

"What are you getting?" I asked him as he was going through the drawers.

"A knife. I want to keep it on the nightstand just in case," he said as he picked a large shiny knife out of the drawer. "One more thing." He walked to the door and grabbed a chair nearby and jammed it under the doorknob.

"Paranoid much?" I asked him.

"We can't be too careful, especially with you here. I have no idea who was in here or has a key," he said to me as he began to shut off the lights. "Come on, baby. I need to hold you."

We crawled into bed and embraced each other in silence. There was no television for background noise, no guys laughing in the living room being obnoxious, just silence. I snuggled against Kayden, wrapped my body around his, and enveloped him until he fell asleep.

I woke to Kayden's voice. He was talking to someone on the phone. "No one contacted me. When was it auctioned off?" he asked. I heard the sound of his fist slamming down on the kitchen table out of frustration. Kayden muttered a few more words before he appeared in the bedroom doorway.

"What happened, sweetheart?" I asked, rubbing my eyes.

"They towed my truck, and when I never contacted the towing company, they auctioned it off last week." His face was pale, and he looked like he was going to be sick.

"We'll figure something out. Fucking shit, it's all because of me," I said as a tear streamed down my cheek.

"Just another fucked-up thing in my life. Thank God for you, Sophia. Come on. Let's get the fuck out of this place. I want to go see Bourbon," he said, holding out his hand to me.

I got dressed and put on my makeup while Kayden went to the mailbox to see what had accumulated since the guys had left. As he rifled through the pile, a pink envelope fell on the table. It was addressed to him, but I didn't see a return address.

"What is it?" I asked him out of curiosity.

"I don't know, but it's to me. There's no address, but I know the handwriting," he replied with a hint of anger.

"Do I even have to ask?" I knew at that moment that he hadn't been entirely truthful. Lisa was still a problem, a thorn in my ass. *Why didn't he tell me?*

"Yes, it's Lisa's handwriting. I didn't think she

226

knew where I lived. I have been so careful about never letting anyone have this address. My mother doesn't even know where I live," he said to me as he flipped the envelope over and ripped it open.

A picture was the first item to fall. It was a photo of two people, Kayden and Lisa, the same fucking photo she texted me many months ago. He pulled out a card, and a letter fell, landing on top of the photograph. I didn't move to pick it up. I didn't even like having the image of that photo in my mind, let alone the contents of a letter. Kayden grabbed the letter but didn't open it. He opened the card and sat in silence as he read the message.

"Is it from her or one you sent her?" I asked him, pissed off.

"It's from her." He looked stunned and worried.

"What did she say?" I could feel my heart starting to pound harder in my chest.

"Read it," he said, handing me the card.

Kayden,

I'll find you...no matter where you are. You're MINE, and I'm yours—always. We're meant to be together. You can't deny fate or destiny. We'll be together again... I promise you.

Love Always,

Lisa

The bitch couldn't take a hint. She was relentless like a rabid dog unwilling to stop. "What's in the letter?" I asked him, still holding the card in my hand.

"It's a letter I wrote to her," he said to me, putting the letter back in the envelope with the photo.

"I don't want to read it. I can only imagine what it says. I'm sure you declared your undying love for her, and now she's reminding you." I threw the card on the table. "Kayden, she isn't going to stop. She'll always be between us. You need to stop her. That is the only way right now," I told him as I reached in and pulled out the pink envelope.

I had to try to put Lisa out of my mind. I needed to convince him to share her messages with his probation officer. She just couldn't be allowed to torment him this way. She had played enough games, but she wouldn't come out the winner. I needed to get that photograph out of my mind, and I needed coffee.

We headed to the French Quarter and straight to Café Du Monde. New Orleans had grown colder since we'd last spent time there. The coffee helped warm my hands as we strolled down Bourbon Street. A loud noise caught my attention and drew my eyes down the street.

Police cars and motorcycles cleared the way and led a procession of people down Bourbon. Above the roar of the motorcycles, I could hear the faint sound of a Dixie band. "Look, Kayden," I said as I pointed down the street. He grabbed my arm and moved me onto the sidewalk and out of the path of the oncoming crowd. "What is it?"

"It's a wedding. Sometimes weddings march down

Bourbon just as they do for a funeral. They're all celebrations of life," he replied while holding my hand.

I watched, riveted to the scene in front of me. A parade of people danced down the street, following the band on their journey. The bride wore a mask and carried a white umbrella, and the groom had on his tuxedo with a matching black mask covering his eyes. They laughed and danced as they proceeded down the street. The wedding guests followed behind, cloaked in similar facial masks, dancing and singing. People cheered on the sidewalk as the parade moved down the street. At the end of the parade, two sets of parents were carried in a rickshaw, waving their hankies in the air, and smiles decorated their faces.

"Wow, I've never seen anything like it," I said as I stared down the street, watching the wedding disappear into a sea of people.

"It's uniquely NOLA, one of the many reasons I fell in love with this city," he said, and I felt his sadness about leaving here. It was like losing an old friend.

* * *

We wandered around the city for the entire day, taking in the sights, sounds, and smells. The memories would have to carry us until we could afford to come back someday. New Orleans had become a second home, filled with memories, both good and bad. We made plans for Mardi Gras months ago that wouldn't come to fruition anymore. My heart ached the more we walked. I wanted Kayden with me, but not by force, by choice. His phone rang as we walked by the casino.

"Hello."

I watched him intently. He received very few calls, and usually, they were only to deliver bad news. I nervously waited to hear what the person wanted from him.

"Okay, I understand," he said before ending the call.

"What's up, baby?" I asked.

"It was Dean from the office. They want to clear the apartment tomorrow." Kayden looked like he had just lost his family pet. I could always read his eyes. They were so expressive and the windows to his soul.

My heart sank. I wasn't ready to leave New Orleans. I thought we could ring in the New Year here in Jackson Square. "It's okay, baby. I know we wanted to stay a little longer, but we can leave tomorrow."

He wrapped his arms around me and tucked my head under his chin. "I'm sorry, Sophia. I wanted this trip to be so much more. I didn't think we'd have to leave so soon. I thought we had a couple more days."

I wrapped my arms tighter around his body and buried my face in his neck. My eyes filled with tears knowing this was truly our last night in New Orleans. "Take me home, Kayden. Make love to me in the bed where you first made love to me."

We couldn't take the bed with us in my tiny SUV. It would be another casualty Kayden would suffer.

We rode in silence, hand in hand, through the streets of New Orleans. Kayden stared out the window, resting his cheek on his hand. I didn't speak. I wanted to give him time with his thoughts.

The apartment felt lifeless as we walked through the door. It was entirely opposite to the lively atmosphere I had experienced during my previous trips. We kicked off our shoes, leaving them by the door, only the thud of them hitting the baseboard filling the room. Kayden grabbed me, lifted me into his arms, and carried me into the bedroom.

He placed me on the bed gently, the hallway light illuminating the room. Kayden lay down next to me, propped on one arm. Looking into my eyes, he cradled my face in his hand. He leaned over slowly and touched his lips to mine. My body tingled, coming to life, and a sense of need filled my veins as his tongue caressed my lips. The tip of his thumb pressed the corner of my mouth and gently opened me to the invasion of his tongue.

Kayden possessed my mouth, controlled my every thought and feeling. He lifted himself off me, leaving his thumb near the corner of my mouth. His eyes never left mine as I captured his digit between my teeth and enclosed it between my lips. He watched me intently as he stripped off his shirt. I sucked his thumb, swiped my tongue across it, and pretended it was his cock. I moved my head forward and back, giving me the ability to suck the entire length. His eyes glazed over before closing, reveling in the sensation. I stared at him as he used his free hand and feet to pull off his pants. His cock sprang free, hard and glistening, the tip weeping.

I pushed him onto his back, releasing his thumb. I needed to taste him. I licked his lips slowly before dragging my tongue down his neck to his torso. My tongue traced each ripple and muscle on his taut stomach. I paused at his hips and bit and sucked the sensitive spots, making his body quiver. His cock nudged my chin, calling for my attention. Keeping my eyes glued to his, I licked the tip. Kayden tasted of salty sweetness, a taste uniquely Kayden—one that I craved. I swirled my tongue around the tip, and his hips bucked as I pulled his length inside my waiting mouth. He filled me, stretching my lips. The hardness of his cock and the softness of his skin moved across my tongue and caused wetness to seep from my pussy. His cock nudged the back of my throat, causing me to gag.

"Fuck," Kayden said. "I love when you gag on my cock, baby."

My face flushed with his praise, but embarrassment filled me at the knowledge I couldn't fit his entire shaft in my mouth. I wrapped my hand around his hardness and moved it in rhythm with my mouth. I squeezed slightly as I reached the tip and drove back down with force. I twisted my hand and flicked the top with my tongue to change the sensation as Kayden neared the edge.

He reached down and grabbed my hair. "Baby, stop. I. Want. To. Make. Love. To. You," he forced out as I sucked him harder and deeper than I had before. Each word stammered out as I reached the tip of his cock.

My mouth released his tip, causing a popping sound to fill the air. Kayden grabbed my arms and dragged me up his body. His hair scraped my skin. He rolled us over, his full body weight crushing me. He plunged his tongue into my mouth, claiming me. His hand slid down my skin and captured my breast in his palm. His lips broke from mine, traveled down my body, and sucked me into his mouth. Overwhelming need consumed me. I needed to feel his cock inside me —filling me completely.

"Kayden, please," I begged.

He licked my breast, circling my nipple with his tongue, which caused my back to arch in an unspoken invitation. I watched as he pulled his lower lip into his mouth between his teeth, causing the hair below his lower lip to stick out. He rubbed his hair across my nipple, pricking my skin, causing goose bumps to form across my flesh. I moaned, writhing from the feel of his scratchy hair against my erect peak. He captured my nipple and sucked it hard, flicking it with his tongue.

"Please," I moaned.

Kayden slid his hand over my thigh, running the tip of his finger down to my core. I gripped his shoulders to stop from crying out. I needed something... anything...inside me. His finger slid easily inside me as his palm grazed my clit. He moved it slowly, torturing me. I needed more friction, my body so close to release.

He moved his body between my legs, his erection lying firmly against my pussy. He rocked against me and kissed me to muddle my moans. Using his hands, he rubbed the end against my opening, rotating it in a small circle, wetting his cock—my body still not accustomed to his size. Staring into my eyes, he entered me slowly, stopping halfway. He paused, looked at me, and said, "Slow, Sophia. I'm going to make love to you. I want to savor you."

I whimpered as he slid his remaining length inside me. My body stretched to accommodate him, relishing the mixture of pleasure and pain. Kayden moved inside me at a steady pace, never wavering, slowly gliding back and forth. Every nerve ending in my body ignited, his cock the spark lighting the fuse.

Our eyes stayed locked, and his face almost touched mine. Our lips tangled together, but I couldn't close my eyes. I didn't want to miss a moment of him. He reached between us, placed my clit between his fingertips, and squeezed in a pulsating rhythm. My world exploded as my pussy clenched, holding him hostage, my body his prison.

His stroke deepened as his body grew tense. "Sophia..." he moaned, his body shuddering as he collapsed on top of me.

"I love you, Sophia," he whispered in my ear. "Being here, with you now, puts my mind at peace."

"I love you, too, Kayden. I'll always be here for you."

"I'd follow you anywhere. My life is wherever you are, not a specific place, but you. You're my home."

* * *

I opened my eyes, staring at the blank wall in front of me. The same spot where Kayden's television used to sit. I knew this would be our last few hours in New Orleans. This room held so many memories for us. Each trip had been filled with a roller coaster of emotions.

My heart grew heavy as tears stung my eyes. A single tear ran down my face, falling onto Kayden's chest. I didn't wipe it away before it fell, not wanting to wake him.

"What's wrong, baby doll?"

Shit. I'd tried not to wake him.

"Just thinking about how this is our last couple of hours in New Orleans."

Kayden and I jumped at the sound of someone knocking on the door.

"Did they say when they were coming?" I scrambled to find clothes while Kayden slipped on his shorts.

"No."

Kayden walked out of the bedroom, leaving me naked and alone. I dressed as quickly as I could, picking up my clothes from last night. I could hear male voices, but I couldn't make out the words. I didn't hear a door close, but I heard strange noises coming from the next room. Kayden appeared in the doorway.

"They're here to clear out the apartment already, Sophia. We have to start packing and leave too," he said. It was real. We were really going to pack everything up and leave New Orleans behind. "The guys are already clearing the furniture out of the living room," he said.

"Okay," I sighed. I shoved everything I could fit into my suitcase. Kayden walked around the apartment grabbing everything he wanted to take before the other guys could grab it. He carried it all into his room and placed it on the floor.

"Hey, Kayden, you taking your bedroom furniture?" a man yelled.

"Nah, I don't have room," Kayden responded.

"I'm sorry," I said. Kayden shrugged and continued throwing his clothes in bags haphazardly. *Shit, this isn't how I wanted him to leave New Orleans.* I helped him pack everything he owned into large black garbage bags. Cold air filled the apartment, and my body broke out in goose bumps from the wind whipping through the small space. Everything about this ending was bone-chilling and mind-numbing.

Placing the last few items in the SUV, Kayden closed the trunk and looked at me.

"That's it, baby. We're standing in the same spot I first touched you—the day that changed my life." He wrapped me in his arms, cocooning me in his warmth. My body shivered at the memory of his lips first touching mine. "Let's go, sweetheart. I'm exhausted, and we still have a long drive back to Florida."

I watched as New Orleans disappeared in the rearview mirror, a gloomy sky framing the buildings. I gripped the steering wheel, trying to distract myself from the sadness that filled my soul. Kayden reached out, grabbed my hand, and placed it against his lips.

"We'll be okay, sweetheart. We'll be back here someday," he said as he kissed my fingers.

"I know we will. I just want you to be okay. I know how much you love her."

"I love you, Sophia. New Orleans is a place. You're my life." Kayden held my hand for hours, stroking my fingers in a reassuring rhythm. The scenery changed, signaling our miles traveled from bayou to palm trees. We grew more tired the closer we got to my home— our home.

sophia

"COME ON, Sophia. Go in the water with me. Please," he begged as he stood near my feet, blocking my view. The warm breeze skimmed across my body, cooling my skin from the harsh Florida sun.

"Okay, but only to my knees." I held out my hand to Kayden even though I knew he was up to something. "I hate swimming in the ocean, you know that. Don't get any ideas, mister."

"I'd never." He chuckled.

I followed Kayden down to the wet sand, watching the waves until the water covered my feet. I was petrified of the ocean, too many dangers lurked—sharks, jellyfish, and rip currents. He led me, holding my hands, until my knees disappeared under the turquoise liquid. I stopped abruptly, and Kayden's hands jerked from my grip.

"Come here, Sophia." Kayden pulled me closer. I

grabbed on to him and wrapped my arms around his neck. He reached for my legs, wrapping them around him, as he began to walk farther from shore.

"What are you doing?" I asked, my voice laced with anxiety.

"Nothing." He smirked.

"You're going deeper. Stop, Kayden." I dug my fingernails into his skin.

"Just a little bit more. It'll be worth it—you'll see." He bobbed with the waves to keep the water from splashing in my face. My heart raced, and I couldn't stop looking around, trying to see if there were any sharks nearby.

"What're you looking for?" He looked in the water, too.

"Sharks. Can't be too careful."

"You're silly, baby. Nothing is going to get you out here. Well, maybe I will, but that's nothing to be scared of." He smirked at me again, and a tingle ran down my spine.

"What do you have in mind?" I raised an eyebrow.

"I want to be inside you." He pushed his shorts down.

"Here, in front of all these people?" I asked as his hands were moving my bikini bottoms to the side.

"No one can see, and it's mine to do with as I wish. I want my cock buried in you," he replied, trying to concentrate on moving our clothing.

"Oh Lord."

I wrapped my arms around him tighter and placed my face next to his. I knew I couldn't stop him at this point. I felt his cock poking my entrance as I braced myself.

"It's going to hurt, Kayden."

"Take it like a big girl. You know you can and will," he said to me as he tried to move his cock inside of me.

I bit my lip to stop from crying out as his cock moved inside of me—not gliding gently. I let him take what he wanted from me. I tried to keep my attention on the people around us, more worried about them than getting off. I played the news headlines in my head: "School librarian arrested for having sex in public. News at eleven." *Shit.*

"Damn, I love being inside of you," he moaned as he pushed deeper.

"Uh-huh," I responded. The worry had taken all form of language from me. *What am I doing?* A wave crashed over his body, hitting me in the face, ruining everything. I coughed, swallowing some water, trying to spit it out.

"Shit, sorry. I didn't even see that one coming," he said. "We'll finish this later," Kayden said, pulling his cock out of me and adjusting my bikini bottom.

"Let's get you back on dry land, baby." Relief washed over me as we moved toward shore. I clung to him like a lifeline.

* * *

I was cranky and exhausted from the sun. I had been short and snippy with my conversation while I drove. "You're being a bad girl, Sophia. Do I have to teach you a lesson?" Kayden asked. My face heated with his words. I loved when Kayden wanted to play. We often talked about fantasies, and he did try to make mine come true.

"I'm not cranky. You're crazy," I chuckled. I wanted him to teach me a lesson—Kayden's lessons were always sexy.

"I'm going to spank you when we get home if you don't watch yourself." He kissed my cheek.

"Whatever, Kayden." The crankiness left me, and a feeling of excitement filled my body. I loved when Kayden spanked me—it was sexy as fuck.

"Just remember, you asked for it," he said as he turned forward and looked out the window.

Pulling into the driveway, I felt giddy. *Don't seem too eager.* "Gonna teach me a lesson now?" I said with a smirk as I grabbed the car handle and looked into his eyes.

"Just you wait and see," he said as he climbed out of the car. I sat a moment in the car to give him a head start through the door. I climbed out, trying to pretend to be sad and scared, but he saw right through me. He knew I wanted this.

He was waiting for me on the bed when I walked into my room. "Come here," he said, trying to remain serious-looking, but I could see the twinkle in his eyes.

"Kayden, I wasn't bad. I don't think I deserve to be spanked," I said, defying him. I may want this, but he'd have to earn it.

"A spanking is the least of your worries, Sophia. Here. Now," he said, patting his lap. I stood there for a few seconds with my hands on my hips, and we both knew I'd do as he asked.

"Okay, Kayden. Your hand will hurt before my ass does," I said with a cocky look on my face as I walked toward him slowly and stared into his eyes.

"I'm sure it will, but it's worth the sting." He grabbed my shorts and swimsuit bottom and pulled them down to my ankles. He moved me like a rag doll over his knees before I could even react.

I wiggled my ass and struggled against his body. I enjoyed every minute of this. Whack. Whack. I felt it before I saw his hand move through the air. My ass stung a little, unable to prepare for the smack.

"Did that feel good?" His hands caressed my cheeks, soothing the sting.

"No, that kind of hurt." I kept my face hidden from him. I had a grin on my face because the pain was minimal. I was on the verge of laughing. I had no idea why, but I couldn't help myself.

"I'm not done yet." He landed another blow.

I was able to cushion the blow when I felt his hand leave my cheek. This time, my laughter broke through.

He smacked my ass again. I laughed harder, and he smacked harder. It was a vicious cycle that was worth the price. I tried to get off his lap, and he placed his arm against my back to pin me down.

"Stop, Kayden," I said, trying to sound hurt but loving every minute of it.

"Not yet." He began to stroke my ass. The tips of his fingers lightly brushed over my pussy. My body betrayed me.

"You're wet, Sophia. Are you turned on?" His stroke became more invasive.

"No, Kayden," I said, moving around on his legs.

"I think you're lying to me. I don't like when you lie to me," Kayden said as his hand moved away.

I braced myself for the next impact, but nothing. "Are you done?" I asked with uncertainty in my voice. *Smack*—question answered. *Smack*. I bit his thigh. He smacked again, but I didn't let go of his flesh.

"Ouch. That hurts!" he said, spanking my ass quickly as he tried to get me to stop. The more he hit, the harder I bit. "Stop," he yelped.

I released my bite and licked the reddened spot to soothe the sting. "I'm sorry. I didn't mean to hurt you," I said with remorse in my voice, trying to climb off his lap.

"I know, love, it's just a tender spot," he said, helping me off his lap.

I stood between his open legs and leaned forward to kiss him. His hands worked to remove my top, throwing it to the floor. He used his feet to pull my bottoms off fully, leaving me nude. Kayden picked me up and tossed me on the bed. Using my feet, he flipped me over onto my stomach. I loved how easily he moved me around. I felt tiny next to him.

"Ah-ah-ah. Don't move." He climbed on my back and straddled me. "We're not finished. I told you the spanking was the least of your worries, Sophia." He leaned over, saying my name in a slow, deep tone in my ear.

A chill ran down my back. His weight shifted, and I took advantage and quickly flipped over. He grabbed my left wrist and moved it toward the headboard.

"Kayden, what are you doing?"

My hands were being bound. I hated the thought of it. I wanted to touch him.

"I'm still teaching you a lesson. I didn't deserve for you to be cranky and mean to me. Let's not forget about lying to me too, Sophia," Kayden said with a glint of humor in his eyes.

He tied up my arms and legs, making sure they were secure. I yanked the ropes, hoping for one to be loose, but no luck. *Damn.* I looked down at my nakedness, and heat spread from head to toe. I watched as he walked into the closet, searching for something. At that moment, I didn't care what he was getting, I loved staring at his ass. I could never get enough of it.

As he turned, I noticed a silk scarf in his hand. "Don't cover my eyes, Kayden, please. I want to see," I said, pleading with him.

"This isn't about what you want. I told you—

punishment. I know how much you like to watch," he said as he placed the scarf over my eyes.

No matter how hard I begged, he wouldn't give in. He already had the whole thing planned in his head. I closed my eyes, waiting for him to touch me.

I tried to listen to everything. I wanted to know where he was in the room and what he might be doing. I could hear him going back to the closet and moving the doors. Then I heard the drawer on the nightstand open. He gathered an arsenal of items to torture me. My heart pounded as I thought about all the possibilities. I felt the bed dip on the side of me where he sat, and my heart leapt in my chest.

"This may hurt a little, but you'll adjust to the sensation," he said, tracing his fingertips lightly across my breasts.

Goose bumps broke out across my skin. My nipples formed into stiff peaks, begging for his touch. He pinched my right nipple lightly and gave it a slight twist. My core pulsated, wanting to be filled.

"Kayden," I said.

"Shh."

The sound of metal chains filled my ears, but it was softer, more like a thick necklace moving on the bed. I knew the sound of the nipple clamps, even though we never used them. I bit my lip, scared of how they'd feel. I felt the cold metal against my skin, waiting for the pain. I felt the pinch of the metal as he adjusted the clamp. I didn't feel pain, instead, a constant pressure that caused my pussy to clench.

My back arched off of the bed from the sensation as he repeated it on the other side. He grabbed the chain, yanking it to test its hold. The sensation was different than anything else I'd felt. He placed his warm mouth over each hypersensitive nipple. My breath hitched before I moaned from his tongue sweeping across my stiff peak.

I then heard the sound of my vibrator turning on. He touched the vibrator to my nipples, and I jumped. He dragged it down my stomach, finally reaching my clit. He held it in place for a moment, my body twitching, and then started moving it back and forth, causing shockwaves throughout my body. My skin began to dampen, and my heart felt like it would burst. I felt my body tightening, and my toes began to curl when he stopped. *Fuck, not this again.*

"No. Don't stop," I yelled.

"I'm in charge here, my love," he said. I threw my head back down on the pillow in defeat.

A moment later, I felt the tip of the vibrator at my opening. My body ached to be filled as he rubbed it lightly in a circular motion before slowly pushing it inside me.

"I want you to stay just like this. Don't move," Kayden said in a gentle tone.

Where the fuck am I going to go?

The bedroom door opened, and I heard his footsteps on the carpet as he moved down the hallway. Kitchen cabinets opened and closed. I heard the sound of ice plopping into a glass. *Oh, no, no, no.* My breaths came shallow and quick. The bed dipped under his weight, the ice jiggling. The cold made me flinch. Shivering, I moaned from the chill near my belly button—my body was aware of every feeling. Everything was more intense. He used the ice to trace a line up my stomach to my breasts, slowly circling each breast in a figure eight pattern. The pattern became tighter and tighter until he ran the ice over my nipples. I cried out, the feeling almost painful. I needed release. The ice moved down to my stomach and then stopped for a moment. My breathing increased as the ice touched my clit.

"Be a good girl, Sophia, and stay still. When I get back, the vibrator better be inside you, or your punishment will continue," Kayden said to me as the bed moved and the door opened and closed. Did he just really leave me here?

"Hello?" I said, but he didn't reply.

The shower turned on, and I sighed. Can he really be taking a shower? He left me here tied up, with nipples clamps, and a vibrator inside of me, ready to explode, and went to take a shower. *Fucker.* The sound of water splashing off of his body, hitting the shower walls, filled the air with the hum of the vibrator. I pulled at the restraints, trying to break free, but he'd tied them too tightly. I couldn't get comfortable and tried to move without pushing the vibrator out. I pictured him naked and wet as the feeling almost made my body numb.

I stopped moving when I heard the water shut off. I could hear him moving around in the bathroom, but I couldn't make out what he was doing. All I could do was lie there and wait. A trickle of liquid slid down from my pussy and trickled onto my ass. My skin grew wet and hot.

The bedroom door opened, and I felt his lips wrap around my right nipple.

"Kayden, please," I begged.

"Please, what?"

"I want you inside me."

"Are we still cranky?" Kayden asked as he tongued my nipple.

"No... Please."

"Have you learned your lesson?" he asked. His mouth closed around my left nipple, sucking hard.

"I promise. I won't get cranky anymore and take it out on you." I knew I'd get my way eventually, but I held my breath waiting for his answer.

He yanked the chain attached to each nipple. I inhaled deeply at the feeling. My body was on fire, and I thought I'd lose my mind if he didn't fuck me soon. His hand trailed over my skin until it reached the vibrator, and I wanted it out of me. He slowly turned it and dragged it out of my pussy. My need intensified at the loss of sensation. He lifted my hips and placed a pillow underneath me. I licked my lips, knowing I'd feel his cock inside me. He moved me to get better access.

I waited with bated breath for his cock to fill me. He positioned himself between my thighs and rubbed his cock against my body. He placed his chest against mine and kissed me deeply, controlling me in every way. He commanded my body, filling my senses. He slowly pushed his cock inside as my core adjusted to the intrusion. Our bodies fit together perfectly.

"Kayden, don't stop. Fuck me," I moaned.

I heard the vibrator again, and I licked my lips with the thought of an orgasm. He placed the vibrator against my clit and began to move, picking up the pace. My entire body tightened, and my arms strained against the ropes as my toes curled. All of the muscles in my body ached, and my skin was covered in a fine sheen of sweat.

Suddenly, my mind went blank. The orgasm was overwhelming. Holding my breath, I felt my head jerk off of the bed. The ecstasy rolled through me in waves. His body tightened between my legs, all of his weight on top of me. He stilled and started to move again as he found his release.

He shifted his weight, kissing me on the lips, cheek, and forehead with tenderness. His body moved away from mine, and I felt his hands against my breast. I held my breath, waiting for the pain I thought would come with the release of the clamps. Removing the clamps, he placed his mouth around each nipple, soothing them as the blood rushed back to places that were deprived. He untied my arms, rubbing my aching muscles. I lay there for a moment, waiting for my body and muscles to adjust after he freed my legs. Kayden grabbed me like a rag doll as he rolled onto his back. I curled into him and swept my fingers across his chest.

"I love you, Sophia," he whispered against my hair. "Have you learned your lesson, love?"

"Yes. I did," I replied with a smile plastered across my face, thankful he couldn't see me. I had learned that I wanted more, and I'd misbehave again for the fun of it. I loved that Kayden wanted to push my boundaries and make my fantasies a reality.

THIRTY-THREE

kayden

NOW, WHAT?

I STARED AT THE SCREEN, reading the message over and over again, unable to really believe the words. I had been invited to interview for a position with UPS. The background check would be ordered if I was selected as a candidate for hire.

Could I pass it?

The judge had said that my record would be wiped clean as soon as I finished paying restitution because I had no criminal history prior to that night.

"Sophia, I got an interview." I tried not to sound too excited, but for the first time in a long time, I thought I had a shot at landing this job.

"Really, where?" She set down her book and turned toward me.

"With UPS. Do you think I have any chance of being hired?" I asked her. "I don't want to get my hopes up. They haven't done a background check yet."

251

"Their requirements may be different, so it's worth a shot. Worst that'll happen is they tell you no," she said to me. She was right, and I knew it. I had nothing to lose.

"You're right. It's on Saturday. Can you drop me off?" I asked her.

"Yes, baby. I'll bring you to the interview. I'm so excited," she said with a smile, bouncing up and down on the bed. "Maybe things are finally starting to turn around."

"It's a nice thought. I'll ask at the interview what their requirements are," I said, trying to think how to broach the topic of my arrest at the interview.

* * *

Sophia dropped me off at the door, but I felt like a slob. Some people wore suits, but others were more casual than me. I didn't own a suit and didn't have the money to buy one for interviews. I pieced together some clothes I salvaged from New Orleans, gray pants and a golf shirt. The line stretched out the door, and I took my place at the end.

Me: Fuck, there are a lot of people here.

Sophia: Don't worry baby. They're hiring for all locations in the Bay area. There's plenty of work to go around. They're going to love you.

A man stepped outside, cupping his hands around his mouth. "The interview process today will take between two to three hours. If you can't stay for that length of time, you can leave now." Some men stepped out of line and walked to their cars. I felt sick waiting in line. My nerves were on edge. I didn't want to talk about my arrest, but I needed to know my chances of landing this job.

Me: A guy just announced I'll be here around 3 hours. I'm sorry, beautiful.

Sophia: That's fine. I'll go shopping. Stay there and knock their socks off, sexy.

I made my way through the various stations and paperwork checks. I sat in the small room, shaking my foot uncontrollably, and waited to be called by the head of Human Resources. I kept debating possible ways to ask about the background check without sounding like a lifelong criminal.

"Mr. Michaels?" a woman called from the doorway. I blinked, taking a moment to realize she was calling my name, stood, and followed behind her. The interview started relatively well. She read over my application and questioned me about my work experience. While I spoke, she flipped through my paperwork, stopped at a spot, and began to tap her pen.

"I see here, Mr. Michaels, that you've been arrested. Tell me about it," she said.

My palms began to sweat as I rubbed them together, thinking before I answered. "I was arrested and charged with criminal mischief."

"Is it a misdemeanor or a felony?" she asked. She chewed on her pen as she waited for my answer.

"Misdemeanor, ma'am," I answered as my heart pounded violently in my chest.

"Were you found guilty?" she asked with a raised eyebrow.

"No, adjudication was withheld," I responded.

"It shouldn't be an issue, then. Misdemeanors are often overlooked, but felonies are the kiss of death." She quickly read over the rest of my application. "Look for an email in the next twenty-four hours. The candidates we've chosen to move forward will receive an email with instructions." She stood up and extended her hand to me.

"Thank you, ma'am. I look forward to that email," I said with a wink. I could usually charm the panties off any woman, but today, my goal was a job. She blushed, and I shook her hand lightly and smiled. I felt confident I would get that email. I always interviewed well with women.

I left the interview feeling upbeat and found Sophia waiting for me in the parking lot. She smiled as I entered the car. "How did it go, sweetheart?" she asked as she leaned over for a kiss.

"Really well. I actually think I got the job, as long as I can pass the background check," I said, rifling through the papers they handed me during the interview. "I'll get an email tomorrow if I'm selected to move forward in the hiring process."

I became obsessed with my email. I wanted this job. I needed it. Every time my phone dinged, I jumped to check it. Just when I was about to give up hope, it arrived.

"I got it, Sophia," I said, still slightly in shock. "I have to fill out the background check agreement and take a drug test."

"Congratulations, baby. You'll get it. I just know it." She wrapped her arms around me and placed a kiss on my cheek.

"I have ten days to submit the background check and get the drug test." I read off the email confirmation. The possibility of being denied still weighed heavily on my mind.

sophia

THE FUTURE

"OPEN IT," I said, watching him tap the envelope from UPS on the countertop.

"I'm scared, Sophia... I want it so badly."

I grabbed the envelope. "I'll open it, then," I said.

"No," he said, tearing open the envelope. He read the pages without speaking, and I couldn't tell from his face what it said.

"Well?"

"Wow," he said with a look of disbelief, still staring at the papers.

"What?"

He was making me crazy.

"It shows no criminal record of any kind. It doesn't even show an arrest," he said as he stared at the pages.

"Does that mean you have the job? Did they search Florida?"

"Yes, I'll be hired. The FBI did the search, and they

looked everywhere in the United States—driving record and criminal," he said, a smile creeping across his face.

Kayden dropped the papers, lifting me into his arms. I laughed as he turned in a circle, kissing my face. The excitement radiated off him and became infectious. "I can't believe it, Sophia. I have a job— finally a job. I can feel like a man again," Kayden said. Tears of joy formed in his beautiful green eyes.

"You've always been a man, Kayden. My man. You've never changed in my eyes. When I need you, I'm sure you'll be there to help and protect me. That's what people do when they love each other. We're a team, and you'll never be alone again," I said, holding his chin so he could look into my eyes.

"I love you, Sophia. I don't know what I did to deserve such a wonderful woman in my life," he said as a tear slid down his cheek.

My heart melted with his words. I kissed his lips and wrapped my arms tighter around his neck. Kayden had been lost for months—always there for me physi- cally, but his mind was elsewhere. He needed a purpose in life.

"Kayden, I'm blessed to have you in my life. You've definitely brought excitement and new experiences," I said into his shirt. I thought about all the possibilities he had now that he was clear of the charges. It meant he could go back to New Orleans. The thought of losing him caused my stomach to twist in knots.

Would he go back to that glorious city and the work he loved so much, or would he stay with me and start a new beginning?

"Kayden, you know that means you can go back to NOLA and your old job. Do you want to go back?" I said to him as I backed away so I could see his face when he answered.

"Sophia, I'm not going anywhere. I can't be without you for a couple hours, let alone weeks. How could you even think I could just pack up and leave you behind?" he asked as he stroked my cheek with his hand, looking like I just stabbed him in the heart.

"I know you loved that job and you miss New Orleans. I just thought maybe—" His finger touched my lips, stopping me from finishing the rest of the sentence.

"Yes, I love New Orleans, and maybe we can move there someday. But you're my home, Sophia. I need to be with you. I want to be with you. I need you to sleep in my arms each night and make love to you each day," Kayden said as he stepped closer and embraced me. I exhaled, not realizing I had held my breath waiting for his answer.

"I just want you happy, Kayden. I want you to be at peace. I know you've struggled with happiness over the last few months." Concern and worry filled my voice, and the feeling nearly suffocated me. He had become my world. We did everything together. I didn't know if I could even function without him anymore.

Could I go back to evening web chats and text messages as our main form of communication? I didn't want to find out the answer to that question.

"I'm staying. End of discussion. I'd never leave you. You're the most important thing in my life," he whispered against my lips before he kissed me. My knees grew weak from the passion and emotion he conveyed with his kiss.

sophia

A NOISE STARTLED ME, waking me from my dream. My heart pounded in my chest. I felt someone staring at me. I had drifted off to sleep hours ago. I could see a fuzzy black figure standing at the end of our bed. My breath came faster, knowing the person had been watching me sleep. My heart pounded so hard I could almost hear it.

"Hello?" I said in a whisper, my hands shaking. I didn't know what else to do. I had nowhere to run. The doorway was behind them, and I was naked.

"He's mine, Sophia," she said in a calm, even tone.

I covered my mouth with my hands as alarms went off in my head—Lisa. She was batshit crazy, and I was alone with her. I squinted, trying to get a better look. I could see something in her hand, but I couldn't make it out. A lump formed in my throat as I lay in the dark waiting for her to act.

"He doesn't want you, Lisa," I said through trembling lips.

"You bitch! What makes you think you can take Kayden from me?" she said in an acidic tone. I could see her figure start to sway a bit.

"Lisa, you threw Kayden away a long time ago. I didn't take him from you." Butterflies formed in my stomach. Should I have told her she could have him?

"I didn't throw Kayden away, Sophia. I was seeing him until you came into his life. I went to New Orleans and spent time with him." Lisa started to move from the foot of the bed.

"Lisa, you had him arrested. You ruined his life. He loves me," I said as I started to shift in the bed. I needed to get away from her. *Think.*

"He'll always love me. Kayden and I were meant to be together. You just occupied his time. You were his bank. He used you," Lisa said, moving closer to my side. She switched on the light and momentarily blinded me. I reached for my glasses, and she swatted my hand. "I didn't tell you to move," she said as I whimpered from the sting.

"I just wanted to grab my glasses," I replied.

She grabbed my glasses off the nightstand and tossed them on the bed and into my lap. I grabbed them and pulled the sheets up over my chest. I sat up slowly, sliding on my glasses. I saw a gun in her hand —she didn't want to talk.

Was she going to kill me?

"Kayden and I have a long history. He loves me and always will. He begged for my forgiveness. He said he couldn't live without me. Kayden always comes back to me," she said as she sat down next to me on the bed. I shook my head as she spoke. They were like fire and gasoline when together. But now, Kayden loved me. He picked me. I didn't believe a word that was spewing from her mouth.

"He's not coming back to you. He's erased you from his heart," I said through a clenched jaw, unable to hold my tongue.

I saw her hand move quickly, and then everything went blurry. I felt a searing pain in my cheek and heard a loud crack. I winced in pain, and my heart began to thump so fast I thought it would burst from my chest.

"Kayden isn't here with you right now. He doesn't want to be with you. Where is he?" she asked.

I sat back up, gathering my hand into a fist. "He went out with friends after work," I said through tears. The pain had faded, but I didn't want her to know.

"He'd rather be with friends than home with you. Don't you see he's not happy with you, Sophia?" The sound of pity was oozing out of her.

I punched her squarely in the jaw, and my fist crunched against her bone. Her head flew to the side, and I jumped from the bed and headed toward the door. She grabbed my hair before both of my feet touched the floor. I continued to move forward, my scalp throbbing as I tried to resist her attempt to stop me. She hit me in the side of the head so hard that I saw different colors dance in my vision. More tears formed in my eyes, and I fell back on the bed, dizzy from the impact.

I blinked a couple of times, but without my glasses, I couldn't see worth shit. My eyes adjusted slightly, and the gun filled my line of sight. "I'm taking him with me. You'll see who he chooses. Don't move or try to fight me. I won't hesitate to shoot you," Lisa said to me, waving the gun in my face. My body trembled as I tried to slow my breathing.

I heard a key in the front door—Kayden.

"Sophia, are you still awake? You left the door unlocked," Kayden said from the living room. My heart pounded as I heard his footsteps in the hall. I could see his figure enter the doorway, and he froze. I held my breath and tried to feel around the bed for my glasses.

"What the fuck are you doing here?" Kayden said in a seething tone, his veins popping out on his neck. All I could do was sit there and stare. Every muscle in my body felt like rubber.

"You're mine. You belong to me and with me, not Sophia. We're meant to be," she said, standing on the side of the bed.

"No, Lisa. We ended long ago," Kayden replied.

"It can be like we were before. I know you still love me." Her face grew red.

"I don't love you anymore. I love Sophia," he

replied quickly as Lisa moved toward him. "Stop right there! You drove me mad and had me arrested. You ruined my life and played with my emotions for the last time!" Kayden yelled at Lisa.

She stepped closer to him, blocking my view.

"Lisa, please leave us alone...please. You have a boyfriend. You don't want me or need me in your life," Kayden said in a softer tone, probably seeing the gun for the first time.

"If I can't have you, Kayden, then neither can she," she yelled, pointing the gun at him.

"Lisa, this isn't you. Put the gun down. Leave now, and we won't call the police," Kayden said.

"Without you, I am nothing."

Lisa tried to kiss him, and my blood boiled. I lunged off the bed and landed on her back with a smack. I wrapped my hands around her neck and squeezed.

"Stop," she said, gasping for air.

"No, Lisa, let go." Kayden fought for the gun, trying to pry it from her grip. A large bang echoed through the air, and my heart stopped at the sound, but I felt no pain. Our bodies fell to the floor in a heap of human flesh. I gasped for air. My mouth was wide open like a fish out of water, winded from landing on Lisa's back. She was crying.

"Kayden," she yelled. "Get up, Kayden!"

Kayden was lying on the bedroom floor, a red spot growing on his shirt. She fucking shot him. I covered my mouth, trying to hold back a scream. She killed my Kayden. I'd finally found a man who loved me the way I wanted to be loved, and this vile bitch took him from me forever. She still hovered over his body, crying and touching his face. She kissed his cheek and pleaded with him to wake up. Bile rose in my throat. *Quiet. Be quiet.* I grabbed a large crystal candle holder from my nightstand and tiptoed behind her.

"You bitch," I yelled, bringing down the candle holder on top of her head. Her body slumped over him. I didn't know if she was knocked out or dead, but I didn't care.

I grabbed my phone, dialing 9-1-1 as I kicked her body off his. His breathing was shallow, but he was alive. "Kayden, hang on. Help is coming," I pleaded with him. "I love you, Kayden. Don't leave me." I sobbed in a shaky voice. My hand shook as I stroked his face, and my lips quivered as I kissed him. I loved him, and he couldn't leave me.

"Sophia..." Kayden said in a shaky voice as I rested my head on his chest, listening to his heartbeat.

"Oh, Kayden! Help is coming, stay with me. Fight, Kayden, please," I begged him. I bit my lip and stared into his beautiful green eyes, the same ones that had captured my attention the moment I saw him.

"I love you, always," Kayden said in a trembling voice. I whimpered as his eyes closed. The color and liveliness he had brought into my life was slipping away from me. I rocked back and forth a bit, mumbling and trying to hold him in my arms. *Where the fuck are the paramedics?* Helplessness and despair sucked the air from my lungs.

I yelled and sobbed as I heard the paramedics rush through the door. I sat back on my feet, rocking and watching them work on his body. Everything moved in slow motion. I heard the men talking, barely able to process the words, Kayden's heartbeat sounding on the machine.

"He's critical, but alive." My heart fluttered in my chest hearing those words, and I bit my bottom lip.

"She's alive," said a paramedic, checking Lisa's pulse.

I hadn't killed her, but she would've killed me. If she could shoot Kayden, I'd be a piece of cake. I sat with my knees pulled up to my chest and my face buried as I rocked back and forth. Tears were streaming down my face. Kayden couldn't leave me —not now.

I sat in the emergency waiting room covered in blood —Kayden's blood. I stared at the floor, watching my tears splash off the tile. "Ms. Romano?" a man said, pulling my attention away from the puddle on the floor.

"Yes." I lifted my head.

"Mr. Michaels is in recovery. He was touch and go

for a while. The bullet nicked some organs, but we were able to repair the damage and stop the bleeding. He'll be in the hospital for a couple of days, but he should make a full recovery," the man said as he patted me on the shoulder. Warmth spread across my body as my tears flowed heavier.

"Thank you, Doctor. When can I see him?" I asked with a shaky voice.

"Give him a while to wake up. A nurse will come and get you," he replied.

I had no other words, only thoughts of Kayden.

I didn't move. I cried—no, I sobbed. I didn't know if they were tears of sadness or joy. Kayden survived Lisa's attack. He didn't leave me.

I entered his room slowly. He looked weak—he'd fought for his life. The machines beeped in a steady rhythm as I walked toward his bed. Butterflies filled my stomach as I stood over him, looking at his beautiful face. I kissed his forehead, trying to smell him, but his scent was missing, replaced by the antiseptic smell of a hospital. I sat down in the chair beside his bed and held his hand. Resting my cheek against his hand, I closed my eyes, exhaustion overtaking me.

I longed to feel his touch.

THIRTY-SIX

kayden

THE BEGINNING

I OPENED my eyes to a yellow room, beeping machines filling my ears. I could feel Sophia's face against my hand, and I turned my head to look at her. Her expression was peaceful after all she had been through. Everything was because of me. I could have lost her to Lisa, and my life would have been over, forever.

"Sophia..." I whispered, moving my fingers to rub against her cheek. Drool ran down the side of her face. That was my Sophia. I didn't want to startle her. She sat up quickly as if in shock.

"Kayden, I love you," she said. She kissed my forehead, my cheeks, and ended on my lips. "Shh. Don't speak, just rest." Tears ran down her cheeks.

"I love you too. Lie here with me, please," I said. I needed to feel her in my arms. I wanted her to curl up against my side, her spot. I hadn't slept a night without Sophia in over six months.

"I don't know, Kayden. I don't want to hurt you, baby," she said, grimacing.

"Get up here. I need you." I patted the bed next to me, not taking no for an answer.

She climbed on the bed carefully, kicking off her flip-flops, and they fell to the floor with a thud. I let her try to tangle her body around me, but she seemed so uncertain.

"Don't worry about hurting me, just lie with me." She finally stopped and rested her head against my chest. I wrapped my arm around her and kissed her head, inhaling her scent. She fell asleep within minutes. I lay there listening to her breathing, the soft snore escaping her lips. I stroked her arm, relishing the feel of her smooth skin.

Footsteps approaching the bed woke me. Two police officers entered my room, and for the first time in years, I wasn't scared by their presence.

"Sorry to bother you, Mr. Michaels, but we need to get a statement from Ms. Romano," the officer said.

"She's sleeping. Can't you come back another time?"

"No, sir. We need to get something on the record quickly from Ms. Romano."

"I've already given you a statement of what happened. What more do you need?" I asked.

"We need to hear it from her. You weren't home or

alert for some of the events. We need her to fill in the blanks," the officer replied.

"I'm awake," she said in low, sleepy voice. "What can I do for you, officer?"

"We need you to tell us what happened on the night of May thirty-first," he said to her.

She recounted the events—waking up to Lisa standing over our bed, the gun, trying to fight her off, and then the shooting. It was the first time I heard the full story. My heart hurt listening to everything she went through with Lisa. I wished I had gotten home sooner to save her. I squeezed her hand as she retold the story, and she gave me a fake smile. She made the officer aware of the history between the three of us. She wanted all the information to be out in the open.

Lisa had been placed under arrest for the attack on Sophia and my attempted murder.

As the officer walked out the door, I whispered, "I'm sorry you had to go through that, Sophia." I kissed her head. I touched her chin, bringing it up, making her look into my eyes. "I love you. Thank you for saving us both."

"You're free of her. She can't hurt you—us—anymore. I'll love you, forever," she said as she leaned forward, kissing my lips.

"You're mine, Sophia, always. I'll never leave you. Don't ever give up on us," I said against her lips. She snuggled back into my arms. We could move forward with our life. Nothing would tear us apart. I didn't know what the future held for us, but I felt a sense of hope. I wanted a family with her. I wanted to grow old together. I loved being spontaneous and surprising her, as long as it didn't end in handcuffs... Well, at least not those used by the police.

"Kayden, will you tell me about your past? There's so much I don't know about you." She looked at me with big, brown, puppy-dog eyes.

"Where do you want me to start?" I asked, butter-flies filling my stomach. "You don't want to hear everything, Sophia." I cringed at the thought of telling her about my entire past. I knew she'd still love me, but she didn't know the depth of my depravity and addictions throughout the years.

"Start at the beginning. I want to hear everything. I love you no matter what, Kayden. I've earned the right to hear the good, the bad, and the ugly."

epilogue

SOPHIA

Six Months Later...

"THE COURT HAS BEEN NOTIFIED that Ms. Jackson has accepted a plea bargain from the district attorney in exchange for pleading guilty to a lesser offense," the judge stated.

My blood boiled as the judge spoke. I wanted that bitch to pay for everything she did to us and to Kayden, but she took the easy way out. She found a way to have her charges reduced from attempted murder to aggravated battery. The court found her unable to stand trial earlier due to a mental problem and ordered her into treatment, placing her on medication. The court now claimed that Lisa was able to make coherent decisions, and she weaseled her way into a plea deal. Kayden rubbed my hand as I listened to the judge's words.

"Ms. Jackson, you are sentenced to ten years in prison with the possibility of parole in three. Court is adjourned." The gavel hammered down, and there was nothing more to be done. Kayden squeezed my hand, but I felt deflated by the legal system. Ten years seemed unfair for almost killing the love of my life and the hell she put us both through.

The bailiff walked to Lisa and waited for her to stand. Lisa turned slowly, and as she stood to walk, she looked toward us. She grinned at Kayden, and it caused my stomach to lurch and a lump to form in my throat. It was not an "I'm sorry" grin, but an "I'm not done with you yet" one. I'd be at every single parole hearing to make sure that conniving whore stayed in prison.

"I fucking hate her," Kayden said as we watched her walk out.

"She almost killed you, and she only gets ten years? It's unbelievable," I said, standing up.

Kayden wrapped his arms around me, enveloping me in his heat. "We're free of her for a long time, baby doll. We'll do everything we can to keep her behind bars. Don't worry, Sophia."

I nuzzled his neck, closed my eyes, and inhaled his smell, the scent of home. Kayden had become that to me, made me feel all things were possible, and as a team, we could overcome any obstacle. His lips brushed against my temple with a whisper-light kiss that calmed my stomach and made me believe everything would be okay.

"Let's go home. You're looking a little pale, sweetheart. Are you okay?" he said.

I looked up into his big green eyes and smiled. There was no place in the world I'd rather be at that moment than home, wrapped in his arms, the rest of the world shut out. "I haven't felt myself lately. It's just the stress of the trial. I'll be okay now that it's over."

* * *

I stared at the calendar on my desk and tapped my pen against the paper. It had been seven weeks since I'd had my period, and I hadn't even noticed. The craziness of the trial and the stress of seeing Lisa again made it slip my mind entirely. I dropped my pen on my desk and leaned back in my chair before exhaling and closing my eyes. Could I be pregnant, or was something else wrong? I rubbed the bridge of my nose and tried to come to terms with either possibility. I'd given up on any chance of a child long ago, and I thought age had stolen that dream.

I couldn't wait to find out. I needed to know for my sanity and self-preservation. I grabbed my purse and headed for the door. Instead of going to the local bagel shop for lunch, I made a stop at the nearest pharmacy to grab a pregnancy test.

My fingers felt sweaty against the faux leather steering wheel. My heart pounded feverishly in my chest, and I could hear my blood flowing through my ears. Every thought I had was filled with images of a baby and Kayden...a little bundle of joy with green eyes and chubby limbs. My vision blurred from tears as I pulled into the parking lot to find out the cold hard truth. I sat a moment, steadying my breath and wiping my eyes.

My legs felt unsteady as I walked down the aisle. I wanted to be pregnant more than anything in the world right now. I thought I had made peace with being childless, but it always hurt deep down. Every new person I met would ask me if I had children, and my answer was always the same. No, life had other plans for me. Every time I gave that answer, my heart felt like a tiny needle pierced it. It had been turned into a pincushion over the years.

I paid for the test that claimed to be the most accurate and easy to read. "Is there a bathroom here?" I asked the cashier. I couldn't wait to get back to work to find out. I walked to the back of the store with the test in my purse, holding it tightly against my body as if it were precious cargo. I tore open the box as soon as I walked through the door and discarded the box, minus the stick. I followed the directions, placed the cap back on, and put it in my purse for safe keeping.

I sat in my car, staring at the stick for a few minutes before. I placed it on the passenger seat and texted Kayden.

Me: Hey, baby, how's work?

Kayden: Good love, whatcha doin'?

I couldn't tell him. I didn't want him to get excited or start planning in his mind if the test was negative. Kayden wanted a family and always felt it was a possibility.

Me: Having lunch. Are you going to be late today?

Kayden: Nah, I'll be home around five.

I wanted to tell him, wanted him to comfort me, but I thought it would be unfair to him. This was something so very personal for me. Men could have children for their entire life, but at some point, a woman lost that ability forever.

I held my breath as I reached over and gripped the pregnancy stick in my hand, scared to see the result. I slowly opened my fingers one at a time, dragging out my torture and any chance of bad news. My eyes grew wide as the blue plus sign filled the test strip window. My heart stopped as the realization of what I was staring at hit me. I was pregnant...we were pregnant. Large teardrops streamed down my cheeks, plopping onto my dress pants. A sob ripped through me, and I allowed the sound to fill the interior of my car. I didn't know until that moment how much I wanted a child, this child.

* * *

Kayden walked through the door shortly after five. I had cleaned the entire apartment waiting for him to arrive. I couldn't sit still and wanted to tell him, but I wanted it to be in person. "Hey, baby," I said, walking toward him as he kicked off his shoes.

"Hi, love." He kissed me on the lips and wrapped his arms around me. "Are you okay, love? You're sweating."

"I'm fine. I've just been cleaning," I said. "Come sit down for a minute."

"What's wrong? Is something wrong with you?" He sat down as I faced him on the couch. I grabbed his hand, squeezing it before I spoke. "You're scaring me, Sophia."

"Oh, sweetheart, don't be scared," I said. "I'm pregnant." A grin crept across my face as I watched his reaction.

His beautiful eyes grew wide. "Really?" he asked. I nodded my head yes, and his eyes glistened with newly formed tears. "Oh my God, I can't believe it." He reached out and placed his hand on my belly. "We're going to have a baby."

"I still need to make a doctor's appointment, but I'm late, and the pregnancy test I took today said I am." I placed my hand on his and leaned forward, kissing his lips.

Kayden wrapped me in his arms, smothering me

with kisses. His lips broke from mine as he held my face between his hands. "A baby. You're giving me a baby. You've made me the happiest man in the world. I love you, Sophia."

"I love you too, Kayden. You've given me the greatest gift in the world," I said, staring into his eyes. Kayden still had the ability to steal my breath like he did the first time he kissed me. Navy blue had been wiped out and replaced by a rainbow of colors. Kayden had filled my world with the color I'd lacked, and now a piece of us would be entwined forever in the form of a child.

* * *

Dear Readers,

Thank you for reading Untangle Me. There's two choices to go from here: Grab **Kayden** to read about the insanity that was Kayden before he met Sophia *or* download **Throttle Me** to find out what happens to Suzy and the beast of a man she hooks up with.

Untangle Me holds a special place in my heart. It's the first full-length book I'd ever written and although my writing has changed over time, I still love Kayden and Sophia's bumpy journey to finding love.

Sincerely, Chelle Bliss xoxo

LOVE SIGNED PAPERBACKS?

Visit *chelleblissromance.com* for signed paperbacks and book merchandise.

ABOUT THE AUTHOR

I'm a full-time writer, time-waster extraordinaire, social media addict, coffee fiend, and ex-history teacher. *To learn more about my books, please visit menofinked.com.*

Want to stay up-to-date on the newest
Men of Inked release and more?
Join my newsletter at *menofinked.com/news*

Join over 10,000 readers on Facebook in Chelle Bliss Books private reader group and talk books and all things reading. Come be part of the family!

Where to Follow Me:

f facebook.com/authorchellebliss1

instagram.com/authorchellebliss

BB bookbub.com/authors/chelle-bliss

g goodreads.com/chellebliss

tiktok.com/@chelleblissauthor

a amazon.com/author/chellebliss

twitter.com/ChelleBliss1

pinterest.com/chellebliss10

be in the know...

Want to be the first to know about the next Men of Inked? Join my newsletter by <u>tapping here to sign up</u> or visit *<u>menofinked.com/inked-news</u>*

Want a place to talk romance books, meet other bookworms, and all things Men of Inked? Join Chelle Bliss Books on Facebook to get sneak peeks, exclusive news, and special giveaways.

Men of Inked
MYSTERY BOX
DELIVERED EVERY 4 MONTHS

SPECIAL EDITION PAPERBACKS &
EXCLUSIVE MERCHANDISE!

CHELLEBLISSROMANCE.COM

Visit chelleblissromance.com to learn more!

acknowledgments

There are so many people who have supported me on this journey and are worthy of praise and my thanks.

I want to thank my amazing beta readers who have held my hand and pulled this emotional story out of my mind. My fantastic beta readers, in no particular order: Deb Schultz, Mandee Migliaccio, Chris Letts, Krystyn Katsibubas, Melanie Lowery, Antionette Smith, Janet Breton, Angie Johnson, Tonya Mabe, Michelle Jeston, Nikki from Blissful Bookblog, Vicki Jones, Christina Omar, and Jacqueline Russell. I love all of you hard.

Thank you to Pepper Winters and Skye Callahan for helping me through the crazy journey that is writing. I enjoyed every moment I was able to join your writing sprints and the moral support. I adore you girls.

Printed in the USA
CPSIA information can be obtained
at www.ICGtesting.com
LVHW032323091023
760634LV00010B/484